# LIFESPAN
## OF A
# MEMORY

LIFESPAN OF A MEMORY: Hearts Out of Water, Book 2
Copyright © 2015-2019 Annie Cosby.

Published by Snowy Wings Publishing.
www.snowywingspublishing.com

Cover designed by Regina Wamba of Mae I Design.
Interior by Key of Heart Designs.
Interior graphics designed by Dover Publications, Inc.
Irish translations by Kevin Ó Maolalaigh.



ISBN: 978-1-948661-25-6
eBook ISBN: 978-1-948661-24-9

Third Edition.

# PRAISE FOR HEARTS OUT OF WATER

# LIFESPAN OF A MEMORY

HEARTS OUT OF WATER · BOOK TWO

ANNIE COSBY

# FOR LUCY

*the biggest scaredy dog I've ever met*
*and, thus, a girl after my own heart*

# PROLOGUE

# *Ag Foghlaim le Fanacht*
## LEARNING TO WAIT

IN THE END, I RAN.

I was scared … confused. High school doesn't prepare you for situations like this! How was algebra or geography going to help me now?

I watched and barely listened as Mr. Hall explained how happy Mrs. O'Leary was at the end. How ready she was. Everyone knew how ready she was. Ready to *go*. It wasn't a lie. But it wasn't the whole truth.

Captain Harville clapped Rory on the back. "She really wanted you to have all this, son," he said. "This will make a great start for you in life."

I watched Rory's face. His beautiful face. It was all innocence and expectation. *He didn't know.* He didn't know any of it. That Mrs. O'Leary was a selkie. Or that Mr. Hall had told me so many scary things in our conversations in The Pink Palace.

What was I supposed to do?

Well, I don't know what I was *supposed* to do. But it wasn't this.

I ran. I said goodbye to that little yellow house that had suddenly become so stifling I could barely breathe. Captain Harville had started an inventory of the books on the shelves, our inheritance, but I picked out *The Selkie Folk* and *A History of Berlin* and told them I wanted to leave the rest to Rory.

"No, Cora—" Rory tried to protest. But I silenced him.

He had done so much work on that house and done so much for that old woman, I said to him out loud. "I think she was your mother," is what I *didn't* say out loud. I couldn't tell him the truth; the least I could do was give him everything else. I held the two heavy books to my chest and rested my chin on them, taking one last look around.

Out on the pier, I said goodbye to Rory. "I'm not ready," I told him. "Not yet. We'll keep in touch." And, of course, I cried. Many more than seven tears.

He kissed me, and I let him. I even kissed back. It was my favorite kind of kiss. The kind where he wrapped his arms around me, holding his hands together on my back so that we were pressed as close as we could possibly be. I interlocked my fingers on the back of his neck, at his hairline where the little cowlick was.

We exchanged emails and promised to message each other, because we wouldn't be able to text internationally. He promised to update me on how the move to Ireland went.

He smiled weakly and tapped his finger on *The Selkie Folk*. "Promise me that one's for a ticket to Ireland. When you're ready."

"As soon as I can take a vacation," I said.

"Vacation." He had repeated the word like it was some kind of vile, offensive term.

"I'll come," I said. My pinky linked around his, I promised.

"There's nothing more binding than a pinky promise," he murmured.

Here was the first boy I'd ever loved, and an old man with a metal detector had come along and tossed a huge secret between us like a grenade. A secret that would change this boy's life forever, if I told him.

St. Louis had a hot autumn and a very cold winter that year. We lost power twice in a series of ice storms. My parents bought me a Hyundai, and I lived at home to attend a community college about twenty minutes away. Mom got me a job at a local flower shop, a favor from one of her many friends. I worked diligently and studied most nights, which was easy to do since Rosie was living it up in a dorm halfway across the country.

Princess had to get stitches and wear one of those ridiculous cone things after a stray cat got a little feisty in the backyard. Dad bought a motorcycle and sold it three months later at Mom's command. Joan started letting her gray hair show after years of dyeing it brown.

In short: life went on.

We emailed exactly three times. He lived with his brother for a few weeks, then found an apartment in Galway, a city on the west coast of

Ireland. He lived with three other boys, all students, and he was studying engineering. But my messages were always eager and pathetic. What was I supposed to write about? Princess's new chew toys? When what I really wanted to say was, "Oh, by the way, I found out you're a selkie. Crazy, huh? Oh, and Mrs. O'Leary is your mom. And you're actually, like, really old." Instead, my responses were shorter each time, and then one day I decided I wouldn't respond. It would be best for the both of us, I told myself.

I'd be lying if I said I didn't cry about it. A lot. All of September, some of October, and then again most of November were tears.

*How had loving Rory been so easy?* What if I'd screwed up my one and only chance at love? What if people spent their whole lives searching for something I'd given away because I was too chicken to have a difficult conversation?

*An impossible conversation.*

That spring, the dentist told me I needed to schedule a day to have my wisdom teeth removed. A brilliant idea struck me, and I picked Valentine's Day. There is no better way to accomplish *not thinking* about something than employing anesthesia.

As if the gods had taken their own personal peek into my heart, the day was overcast and sporadically rainy, just a few degrees too warm to turn it into snow. Mom went with me to the hospital and waited in the prep room while a lady with a very soothing voice gave me the good stuff.

"You'll wake up when it's all over, as if no time has passed at all," the woman was explaining. *Is that what Rory—Ronan—felt when he came back from the sea?*

*Of course not,* I admonished myself, *he was a baby.* As if *that* part of it made perfect sense.

"Your mouth will be sore, but that's it. All okay?"

I tried to reply but a calm that I was finding quite impossible to combat was already settling over me.

"Just relax," the woman said. She had disappeared. I turned my head slowly from side to side, but she was nowhere to be seen. Everything I could see was very wobbly on the edges.

I could see Mom. Her face was scrunched up as if worried, and I tried to tell her I was just fine, that she could go back to the waiting room. But I couldn't hear the words that came out of my mouth. I tried again, but once more, I had no idea what I'd just said.

*I'm sure it was close.* I shrugged.

My eyes felt heavy, but I mustered my strength and pulled them open. I was in a small, dim room. It looked like a closet, really. *Where in the ...* It was taking an insane amount of effort to get any part of my body to move, but I finally got my head to turn. There was Mom. She was sitting next to me; behind her a drawn curtain formed the fourth wall of this tiny room.

*Of course. The teeth. Is it over already?* A pounding in my jaw told me it was. I tried to sit up but the look on Mom's face caught my attention.

She looked like she'd just seen the Loch Ness Monster. Her eyes were wide with fright and she had a hand around her throat as if to strangle some terror out of herself.

"What?" I tried to say. It got caught up on my tongue, which felt enormous. "*What?*" I tried again. *Did they butcher my face?*

"Cora!" Mom glanced anxiously over her shoulder and wrenched the curtain closer to the wall, as if that could keep this conversation from the people outside. "Cora, are you ..." She nodded toward my middle.

"Am I what?"

She nodded more vigorously at my stomach.

"Hungry?" I supplied.

"Pregnant!" she hissed.

"Dear god! What went on in that surgery?" I shrieked. "I thought they were working on my mouth!"

"You were babbling in your sleep!" Mom hissed. "Are you, Cora? You tell me right now! Oh my god, you are! Is *that* why you've gained weight?"

"Gahhh! No, Mom, that's just me!" I groaned angrily. "I'm not pregnant! What the hell did I say in my sleep?"

"You said you needed to tell him!" Her voice dropped to a hiss. "You said you needed to tell him about the *babies!*"

"Him who—oh." *Way to sell me out, subconscious,* I thought, but I said, "Mom, I was on drugs. I was babbling. It was nonsense."

She looked at me for a long moment, loud bursts of air escaping her flared nostrils. "You would tell me—"

"Can we *please* stop talking about this? I'm *not* pregnant!"

"Then what—"

"It's from a book I'm reading! This chick didn't tell her boyfriend she was pregnant ... with, uh, with twins. Jesus, can we please go home?"

It took another few minutes in that little wake-up room to convince my mother otherwise, but I finally got her to believe I was not with child, narrowly escaping the necessity of explaining to her that the real problem weighing on my subconscious was whether or not to tell the boy I loved that he and his brother had *probably* spent a great deal of their lives as baby seals.

*If I was braver, I would have gone with him. I would have run away to Ireland with him and told him everything.* I thought it nearly every night before I went to sleep. *You still can.*

But this wasn't a movie. Who was to say he wasn't dating someone by now? Heck, who was to say he wasn't *engaged?* Married! He could have a kid on the way!

I tried. I tried *hard.* But I was not over Rory O'Brien. It was a rabbit hole of confusion, a broken heart … and guilt.

I had to tell him.

I couldn't keep this secret forever. And at the same time, I couldn't imagine revealing it to anyone. Least of all the person I'd begun to trust more than anyone on earth and, in turn, whose trust I had completely failed.

All of these things I kept to myself. Even Rosie's patience wore thin. "I'll fix you up with some friends of mine," she told me one day near the end of the school year. "You have to keep trying." *Or you'll be alone for the rest of your life,* was the unspoken implication.

But I didn't go out with any of Rosie's suggestions. Because a completely different boy showed up on my doorstep seven days later.

But splash and grow strong,

And you can't be wrong,

Child of the Open Sea!


\- RUDYARD KIPLING

*The Jungle Book*

# *Cuairteoir Neamhthuairimeach*
## AN UNEXPECTED VISITOR

THE DOORBELL RANG, WHICH WAS ODD IN ITSELF. The only people who came to the front door were there to visit my parents, and my parents were in Los Angeles for a week, as all their friends and business associates knew.

"Pause the movie," I told Rosie.

She was home from LNU for the summer, and I had just finished my last exam of the year that afternoon—I'd be happy never to see another calculus textbook as long as I lived.

Instead of doing anything productive like finding Rosie a summer internship or helping each other pick the majors we'd have to declare soon, we'd opted to stuff ourselves with Cheez-Its and Ding Dongs in front of a scary movie while we dished about school. The first year of our college careers had come to an anticlimactic close. Rosie had plenty of frat boys at LNU to tell me about, including one deliciously aloof one named Luke, and I had plenty of really old professors from the community college to bemoan.

The doorbell rang again, and Princess barked in harmony.

"Coming!" I yelled.

"Whoa—you shouldn't go by yourself!" Rosie jumped to her bare feet to follow me to the door, Princess at her heels. "What if it's a freaking ax murderer?"

I rolled my eyes. "We really shouldn't be watching that movie while we're home alone."

Starting to undo the locks, I stuck out a knee to keep Princess from running outside.

Then I opened the door and looked up. And nearly fainted.

"What the—"

My leg fell and Princess bounded outside, jumping as high as she could and licking the newcomer's hand.

There was a boy standing on the doorstep with a forced smile plastered on his face.

"Hi," he said nervously. "It's Aidan." He pulled a hand out of his pocket to point awkwardly at himself as he said, "Aidan O'Brien."

"I ... I ... " *I know it's freaking Aidan O'Brien!*

That wasn't what I was having trouble comprehending. The difficult part was that I hadn't talked to Aidan O'Brien since I left Oyster Beach nine months ago. When you're trying desperately to fall out of love with someone, you don't exactly go around calling his little brother just to chat.

What in the world was he doing at my house? My actual house? The not-pink one?

"I ... what the he—"

"Cora!" Rosie interrupted loudly. "Why don't you introduce us?" It was her full-on flirting voice, all gooey and sugary sweet, and her shiny auburn hair had somehow made it out of the ponytail in place two minutes ago to fall over her shoulders in glorious waves. She was about to flirt with him. With Rory's little brother. Who was in St. Louis. The little brother of *Rory*. My Rory. Or ... *not my* Rory.

"This is Aidan," I said, my mind reeling.

"Yeah, I got that." Rosie threw me a look that said I was acting like a deranged clown and turned to Aidan. "What a cute name." She pushed in front of me and extended her bright pink nails. "Rosie."

"Hi," Aidan said, shaking her hand timidly.

"Why don't you come in?" Rosie suggested, as all functions managed by *my* brain were obviously failing.

As he stepped into the hall, his eyes widened just a fraction of an inch. He looked around him, his cheeks turning slightly red, and dragged his Nikes across the doormat a few too many times. The staircase leading to the second floor was a wide thing, made of ornate wood, and there was a big chandelier hanging above it. I didn't really notice it anymore, but it made an impressive entryway to newcomers, I knew that. What I didn't know was that an O'Brien boy would ever be standing in it.

Rosie led him into the TV room and invited him to sit down, obviously giving me time to regain my senses. He sat carefully on the black leather, his hands in his lap as if he was afraid of touching anything, as Princess sniffed around his feet.

It occurred to me that Rosie wasn't grasping the enormity of this situation. "Rosie, this is Aidan—"

"*Really* starting to sound like a broken record, here, hun," Rosie said, taking a seat next to the visitor and crossing her thin legs at the knees.

"Aidan is Rory's brother," I said pointedly.

Her hazel eyes grew big as dinner plates. "Oh!" she gasped. Of course she knew everything there was to know about Rory. I'd been in tears for most of autumn, so it would have been a little difficult to keep it from her. Aidan, however, had not exactly come up in conversation. After all, I'd only met him a handful of times.

"How … you …"

Aidan was looking at me like he was worried about the state of my sanity, and even Princess looked at me with her head cocked like I was a particularly confusing thing. I wasn't quite sure I would ever recover from this shock, either.

"How?" I squeaked.

"A plane," Aidan said. He rubbed his forehead with the back of one hand, as I remembered Rory doing when he was nervous.

"Right. Of course."

Staring into a smaller, more timid version of Rory's face was giving me a pain like I hadn't felt in months. I'd forgotten how strongly I could feel—happiness or sadness, I hadn't felt anything that powerful in a very long time.

"So … I'm Rosie," my best friend chirped, desperately trying to save the mood in the room. But it was far too late for that. Even Princess looked uncomfortable as she sat at Aidan's feet, ears alert and head cocked.

I had to get my shit together. There was a reason he was here. It probably had nothing to do with Rory. But what *did* it have to do with? Maybe he just happened to be in town … In the great flyover states? Not likely. It had to have something to do with Rory. *Focus, Cora, focus.*

"W-what, uh, what brings you to St. Louis?" I finally stammered, trying to smile at the mini-Rory. He was smaller and thinner than I remembered, but to be fair, my mind had been otherwise occupied the previous summer.

"Mr. Hall died," Aidan said simply.

That was certainly not the answer I was expecting. To see the Arch, maybe. To taste the barbeque, perhaps. But what did Mr. Hall have to do with my life in St. Louis? We hadn't exactly been … er, *friends.*

"I'm sorry to hear that," I said. And I meant it. But I didn't know Aidan O'Brien was that close to the man. My eyes narrowed in suspicion, as if the conniving old man could somehow reach me from the grave, but I tried to keep my voice light, conversational. "How did he—"

"Cora, he told me everything."

*Oh.*

"Everything?" I repeated, my throat going dry. *You mean everything that I learned about your brother but failed to mention to your brother before breaking it off with him and mauling my own heart by leaving and more or less losing all contact?*

I gulped.

Rosie's eyebrows were so high they were getting lost in her side-swept bangs.

Aidan took a short breath. "I know"—here he threw a skeptical look at Rosie—"that my real dad might not be dead. Mr. O'Leary. That he didn't die at sea; he left." Was that it? What about Mrs. O'Leary? What about the *s* word?

Rosie let out a fake chuckle. "Regular soap opera, aren't we?"

I gulped and looked at her nervously. I couldn't talk about this in front of her, not if there was a chance we'd hit upon the more fantastical elements of last summer. Rosie was my best friend, but she was anything but imaginative. "I'm kind of tired, and it's pretty late," I said briskly, hoping he got the hint.

But I noticed then that he had a backpack with him. Of course, what did I expect? That he'd booked a room at the Chase Park Plaza Hotel? "Do … do you need a place to stay?"

His face turned red. "Well, yeah, sort of."

"Well it's your lucky day!" Rosie cooed brightly. "Cora's parents are out of town!"

I started to spin away to prepare the guest bedroom on the second floor for him. It was the smallest and would be the easiest to straighten up and hide the evidence before Joan came to check in on me as she did every few days. Having a boy spend the night wasn't exactly something I wanted to discuss with Joan or my parents. But as I turned, there was still something bothering me. He hadn't actually answered my question. I took a quick breath of confidence and spun back around.

"But, Aidan, why are you here?" I blurted out.

His mouth was partly open, as if he was just about to blurt something of his own. He clamped it shut. A small smile crept across his face and I couldn't help but laugh at the absurdity of our social skills. As his smirk grew, I couldn't push away the thought that it looked just like Rory's.

"I just mean, why did you *really* come here?" I tried again.

"Well," he said hesitantly. "I'm going to Ireland, and I need you to come with me."

# Bain Níos Mó Sult as Do Shaol
## LIVE A LITTLE

I WAS SO TIRED I WANTED TO COLLAPSE, BUT MY mind was far from shutting down for the night. I turned out the light in my room and crept down the stairs. Rosie was in my room (I'd convinced her to wait until tomorrow to hit on Aidan) and Princess was snoring peacefully in her dog bed in the corner. But I knew I had to say something to the surprise visitor before I went to bed.

"Of course we'll go!" Rosie had practically yelled at Aidan after his proposal. I'd been too shocked to say anything at all. Instead, I'd jumped right into finding an extra pillow for the guest, despite the fact that the guest room was stuffed full of pillows of every imaginable shape, size, and density. Even so, Aidan had been polite and quiet, letting me retreat into my own world, which had been rocked on its axis.

But it couldn't stay like that. I had to talk to him.

My socked feet were quiet on the carpet as I crossed the second-floor hall and poked my head into the purple guest room. The door was open, the light was still on, and Aidan was sitting on the striped bedspread, reading a spiral notebook.

For the first time, I saw him as Rosie must have seen him. He was thin and had a dark mystery about him. But maybe that was just because of what I knew. His skin was tan, and his hair was dark brown—though a little lighter than Rory's. His hair was tousled in the way that I had come to associate with the beach, however many miles away we were at the moment. And his eyes—his eyes were big and round and very, very dark brown, like melted chocolate. They looked almost pained now, tiny creases reaching out from the corners of his eyes like wrinkles belonging to a man three times his age. Nonetheless, he looked something like Rory. So of course he was beautiful.

His head bolted up when I appeared in the doorway.

"Anything else you need?" I asked. "I got you an extra blanket, right?"

He nodded. "I'm set."

*Talk to him, Cora.*

"It's just that my mom keeps the air conditioning up really high, it can get kind of cold. Do you want me to turn it down? She'll be gone, so I can—"

"I'm good," he said with a small smile.

"Okay … I guess I'll see—"

"Cora—I … I didn't want to say anything in front of your friend. But, uh … I know about … well, everything."

*Oh, everything.* It came flooding back to me in a heady rush of sand and salt. All of it. Everything. Mrs. O'Leary's inexplicably tender love for Rory. The name. *Ronan.* The fact that she'd been with both babies when they disappeared. The alleged strange aging patterns of selkies. And the one glaring fact I couldn't ignore: there were supposedly three sealskins. Not one. *Three.*

"Everything?" I repeated breathlessly.

"Well I know what Mr. Hall told me."

Which was probably what he'd told me. The truth that I was too terrified to acknowledge. Mr. Hall had given me all the facts and left me to sort through them. If my powers of logic had been working correctly last summer, when Mr. Hall said Mrs. O'Leary had been "ready to go," he didn't mean she was ready to go to whatever great beyond awaits humanity after this mad adventure we call life. What he *really* meant was that she was ready to go put on the sealskin that he'd finally deigned to return to her and transform into a seal. And that was downright mad.

But that wasn't the scariest bit.

Lia O'Leary hadn't drowned her baby boys like most of Oyster Beach thought, that was easy enough to believe. But if Lia O'Leary had sent her beloved Ronan and his little brother back to the sea as seals, where *the human part of him will not age until he walks again on two legs*, as she'd told me, then it was entirely possible that the two boys Seamus O'Leary found years later and had adopted by the O'Briens were actually his sons. *Her* sons. "Ronan," she'd called Rory for years. What if she wasn't nearly as deranged as everyone in Oyster Beach thought she was? The more I'd thought about it, the more it made sense, the pieces falling together like a terrifying puzzle. And *that* was deranged.

"What did he tell you?" I asked breathlessly.

"That Mr. O'Leary was our dad, mine and Rory's. And Mrs. O'Leary our mom."

The blood rushed to my cheeks and I nodded slowly. "Yeah, that's what I suspected," I murmured.

"That would make us …"

I sucked on my bottom lip, willing him to stop talking. I wasn't in the right mind to respond in an intelligent manner. But more importantly, I wasn't sure I'd *ever* be in the right mind for it. That's why I'd left Oyster Beach like a coward in the first place. "Their sons?" I suggested hopefully.

"That. And selkies."

There it was. He'd finally said it. The *s* word. I nodded, visions flitting through my mind of a Mr. Hall rasping secrets on his deathbed. Why couldn't he have kept his damned mouth shut a little longer?

Aidan twisted around and pulled something out of his backpack. It was a leathery length of material. Dry and gray. A little squeak of a gasp sounded in my throat.

Aidan wrapped it around his thin hand like a glove and held it out like he was admiring a jewel. Then he laughed, shaking his head. "You don't know how many times I've tried to uh … put this on … somehow." He looked up at me with that charming O'Brien smirk. The effect wasn't quite the same as Rory's, but it was enough to twist my heart in memory of his brother.

"Is that …"

Aidan nodded, brushing his open palm against the material.

The sight of the skin in his hands made my heart beat faster as the memory of its texture haunted my fingertips. That fateful day in Mrs. O'Leary's cottage, I hadn't seen any sealskins, and I'd been terrified that Rory was gone, too—in my heart knowing, even then, what he was. But then I'd seen it. In my relief, I had held it, dry and scratchy between my fingers. Amidst the confusion and relief of my heart when Rory entered the little yellow house, Mr. Hall had taken the skin gently from my hands, and when my eyes briefly met his, a corner of his lip picked up in a silent goodbye, his hands were clasped behind his back. It was clear: he wasn't going to say anything to Rory. And, at the time, I'd thought, *It's what Seamus would have wanted. It's for the best.*

But now? Mr. Hall had reneged on that silent promise. He'd told. He'd given the thing to Aidan. So now I had to spill all, too.

"Rory told me once, when we were in Seamus's shed, that there were three skins," I said. "One was missing."

Aidan nodded again and met my eyes, the ghost of a smirk on his lips. "Mr. Hall told me he thought it's in Ireland."

"And you want to find it."

He nodded and silence consumed us.

"Did she ever … come back?" I asked softly. I'd had countless dreams over the past months of Mrs. O'Leary reappearing in Oyster Beach, sealskin in hand. And they weren't good dreams. They were dark and stormy and I always woke up in a sweat. And they weren't the only nightmares I had.

But Aidan shook his head, his brown hair falling into his eyes. "No, she's definitely gone."

"Aidan … I don't even know what to say."

"I know. Neither do I. That's exactly why I need you to come with me. I have to tell Rory and I'm not sure I even understand everything and I don't want to do it alone."

My throat constricted. I let my eyes fall to the carpet. It was safer there. Fewer words down there. If only I could live there forever, the size of a mouse.

"I *have* to find the third skin, Cora. The first one disappeared with Mrs. O'Leary and we have this one—that leaves one out there somewhere. I don't know where exactly, but Mr. Hall thinks it's somewhere in Ireland. He also thinks that's where Mr. O'Leary went when he disappeared. It's as good a place as any to start the search."

"That might be a difficult search," I murmured.

"That's why I need your help. And … and I thought maybe you could help me buy a ticket." When I looked up his cheeks were scarlet. "I—I didn't know who else to ask—"

"Of course," I cut in quickly. "You know I have that money from the books—Mrs. O'Leary's books, I don't know why she left *me* money, but you and … your brother—you're the closest descendants. It all belongs to you."

"But, that's not the only reason I came to you, Cora," Aidan said quickly. "I don't want you to think it was just for the money. It's true, I spent my last $250 to get here, but … that's not the only reason."

My eyes retreated back to the soft, creamy carpet where they were safe from any emotion.

"You're the only other person in the world that knows about this, Cora," Aidan went on. "The only one. Well, you know, besides my dad. My real dad. And who knows what Mr. Hall said to you that he didn't get the chance to tell me? I *need* you."

Those were words I'd dreamed of hearing a million times. Words I'd dreamed of hearing from Rory's mouth. Not his brother's. "How did Mr. Hall die?" I asked, just to change the subject.

"Cancer. He didn't tell anyone until this winter when it had already practically killed him and people could tell something was wrong."

"That's horrible," I said softly. Standing awkwardly in the doorway, I felt the first pang of pity for the old man. He'd always unsettled me in life, but in death, I felt sorry for him. For the first time it occurred to me that he wasn't just a spectator—he'd been hurt by this whole selkie thing, too. He'd been deserted by his best friend. Deserted and left with a terrible secret. When Seamus left Oyster Beach, he hadn't just abandoned Mrs. O'Leary. He deserted his best friend, too.

"Cora, can I ask you something kind of personal?"

I shrugged. "No promises I'll answer."

He smiled; it was fleeting. "I was just wondering—you don't talk to my brother any more, do you?"

My heart sank. I knew, of course, that it was going to come up. How could it not? But I hadn't expected him to come right out and ask. "Not really, no." I wondered if—hoped against hope that it was true—Rory had mentioned me.

"You don't—you guys aren't ... I mean, you guys seemed pretty serious last summer."

"Yeah, things just got messy and confusing."

He grinned. "Guess what. Things just got messy and confusing again."

A strangled laugh escaped my throat.

"I'm sorry for prying," he said. "I just thought you guys would at least still be friends."

"We are," I lied. Three emails over the course of a year didn't exactly constitute friendship. But for the good of my still-mushy heart, I'd stopped responding to his emails. As if when the emails stopped, Mr. Hall and the reality of his words would disappear, too. But the thing was, the world had kept on spinning and it had reached May and here I was, clinging desperately to the twirling world, and still thinking about Rory O'Brien every day.

"You don't have to come with me," Aidan said quietly. "But it would be awesome if you did."

I sniffed and nodded. "I'll see you in the morning."

He deflated like a balloon as I closed the door.

Creeping silently into my room, I closed the door as quietly as possible.

"Well?" Rosie demanded from the blackness. So much for being quiet.

"Well what?" I said petulantly. "I haven't decided anything."

"Oh my God, Cora! A really hot guy just showed up on your doorstep asking you to fly halfway across the world with him to go see his equally hot brother!"

"Ireland isn't halfway across the world," I said.

Rosie sighed dramatically. "Learn to live a little, Manchester!"

# *An Cinneadh*
# THE DECISION

I T'S NO SURPRISE THAT I COULDN'T SLEEP. I WOKE up in the wee hours of the morning, torn from the horror of one of my recurring nightmares, and went downstairs. In the time before the nightmare, I'd tossed and turned for hours. And I'd eventually made my mind up about one thing. One gigantic thing.

I poured a bowl of Cheerios and sat down at the marble counter to wait. My stomach was eternally turning over, so I didn't eat much. Just pushed the cereal around with my spoon, watching the tiny O's soak up milk and get soggy. They were just a floating pile of mush by the time I heard footsteps coming down the back stairs that had been a servants' entrance way back when the house was built.

Aidan appeared, his hair even more disheveled than yesterday. Needless to say, it reminded me of Rory. And that glorious night we'd spent together at O'Brien Resort.

"Uh, hi," I said, surprise no doubt showing on my face.

"Couldn't sleep either, huh?" he said, stifling a yawn.

I shrugged and gestured toward the boxes arranged before me like a display. "Cereal?"

"Thanks," he said, sitting down on the cold, metal stool next to me. I watched him deliberate between Cocoa Puffs and my mom's Special K with strawberries. He picked the latter. The road less traveled. Typical Rory move.

I pressed my eyelids firmly together. I'd spent so many agonizing hours deliberating whether or not to do what I was about to do. I didn't need to think about it anymore.

"When are you leaving for Ireland?" I asked quickly.

"Um, I don't have a ticket yet," he said between bites. "I was planning on buying one today, finding an internet café or something. Get the first plane I can."

I nodded. "Of course." I took a deep, calming breath that did nothing but make me feel light-headed. "I … I, uh, I'll go with you."

"You'll *what?*" Rosie shrieked. She was standing in the doorway to the back stairs, fists on her hips, mouth hanging open. Princess clattered down the stairs behind her.

"What are *you* doing up?" I demanded. "Are you aware it's 5 a.m.?" Did she have me wired? Or had she just dragged herself out of bed to get a ridiculous jumpstart on Aidan-hunting?

"Don't change the subject! What did you just say?"

"I'm going to Ireland," I repeated.

Her face broke into a smile, revealing those pearly whites that had spent all of freshman year in braces. "I didn't think you had it in you, Manchester! I'm game!"

"Rosario Balducci, you were not invited," I said with a smirk, using her full name as her dad did whenever he was chastising her. Which, truthfully, wasn't very often.

Rosie raised her perfectly plucked eyebrows and looked to Aidan.

He laughed, a smile splayed across his face. The biggest smile, in fact, that I'd ever seen him wear. One of his front teeth was the tiniest bit crooked, which only made the smile all the more endearing. "The more the merrier!"

We didn't waste any time. The computer in my dad's office was ridiculously old. His laptop had rendered it obsolete, but the printer was still in there. There was a mess of envelopes on the desk that I swiped aside before setting down my laptop and plugging it into the printer. It was dim in here, even with the lights on. Two giant moose heads stared each other down across the room, perched on opposite walls. My dad shot them up north on one of his business trips.

Even the desk chair in here emanated power. Aidan sat in it, a leather rolling chair with a ridiculously high back. He looked like a kid playing at being a grown-up.

"Um, Cora, what exactly are you going to say to your parents?" Rosie asked.

"I'll tell them I'm taking a vacation," I said hesitantly. Telling the truth about Ireland was out of the question; they'd know at once who I was going to see. Considering the amount of crying they'd heard through the floorboards last autumn, they would *not* approve of my flying across the world for this particular boy. And that was *after* all the unapproving they'd done last summer due only to which end of the beach Rory lived on.

But credit card bills wouldn't hide the truth for long. Luckily, neither my mom nor my dad saw the virtue in checking frivolous things like balances very often. The lie should last just long enough. "I'll say we're going to Florida," I said lamely, shoving my debit card at Aidan. "That's an approved Caroline Manchester vacation spot."

"Thanks," Aidan said, his cheeks going scarlet again. "I owe you big time."

"Isn't the drinking age eighteen in Ireland?" Rosie squealed as she ran to her purse for her (dad's) credit card.

"It's your money," I said to Aidan, completely ignoring Rosie. "You don't owe me anything." Aidan brought up a flight search engine and entered all the information for flights going to Dublin this evening.

I pointed at the screen eagerly. "There's a flight in a few hours! That puts us in Dublin by nine p.m.!" My heart beat a little faster. A couple of clicks and it would be set. Was I really going to do this?

"That's in three hours. Do you think we can make that?" Aidan asked skeptically.

If we waited any longer, my chicken spirit would certainly come back to me from wherever it had gone. I couldn't risk that. "What return date?" I said, ignoring his doubt.

"Well," Aidan said, hesitating. "Mine doesn't need … I mean, well, I don't know … maybe I'll be staying longer than you …"

My cheeks felt hot. He was right. How was I supposed to know whether this would go smoothly or whether it would all go to hell the minute we got there? "Um, make mine and Rosie's for … a week?" I suggested.

"How about two?" Rosie chirped, bouncing back into the room.

"Do you know what to do when we get to Dublin?" I asked Aidan. *How to get to Rory,* is what I meant but didn't say out loud.

He nodded. "We'll get a bus to Galway. It's on the west coast."

The confirmation for three tickets in my hand, still warm from the printer, Aidan set about looking up bus times. "Here, write these down."

I grabbed one of the envelopes I'd pushed aside earlier on the desk. It was unopened, but it was thin and the fact that my dad had left it on his desk so long meant it was unimportant. Probably a bill or something. I furiously scribbled down the times Aidan read aloud before Rosie let out a high-pitched squeal, grabbed my hands, and danced me around the room.

"We're going to Europe! We're going to Europe!" she yelled in a sing-song voice.

And the longer we danced, the more my hands began to shake.

When I finally got her to free me, I started making plans. I'd need the neighbors' help. Luckily, one was a postman and would definitely be awake by now. I'd have to get them to watch Princess, who could already tell something was going on. She sat in the doorway to the office, head cocked, tail still, completely aware in that weird doggy sixth sense of being abandoned. And then there was Joan! I'd have to leave a note in case she came to clean or bring me food as she did from time to time when I was staying alone. And the flower shop. I only worked a handful of hours a week, and much of the time there was little work for me to do—it was a flower shop, not the Pentagon—so I could easily call in sick.

And *packing*! I hadn't even thought of that. All those menial things I couldn't forget—like my toothbrush. If things went well, I was going to need a toothbrush. The memory of Rory's warm lips on mine came back to me in full force.

*Oh, please God, let there be need for a toothbrush.*

# *An Mac Eile*
## THE OTHER SON

I T ALMOST FELT LIKE I WAS GOING TO CHICAGO for a weekend away. That is, until we were sitting at the gate in the international terminal at O'Hare, waiting for a big plane to sweep us across the Atlantic.

I'd been on overseas flights plenty of times. My parents regularly went to Germany and Italy, and I'd been to France and Spain with them once. But this was different and my stomach knew it. This was *so* different. This wasn't parent-approved. And not just a parent-unapproved journey to Rosie's or a parent-unapproved concert. This was *big*. My stomach was flipping around like I'd set a bouncy ball loose in there.

Rosie plopped down beside me, holding two sandwiches wrapped in cling wrap. "Are you sure this is the best idea?" she asked, handing me one of the sandwiches.

"What? Airport food? No, it's rarely a good idea, but I'm starving."

Rosie rolled her eyes. "This trip, Cora!"

"What?" I demanded. The last thing I needed was Rosie, my guaranteed push into action, double-guessing things when I was already triple-guessing them. Besides, it's not like we were going to get any trouble from Rosie's dad and stepmom. The Balduccis were as hands-off as you could get when it came to parents. "You're the one who told me to go!"

Rosie threw a glance at Aidan who sat on the other side of me, headphones in and head bobbing ever so slightly. "I know, but … you know, running after Rory when you're just starting to get over him—are you sure that's the best idea?"

Rosie liked to talk about everything. Me? I liked to bottle it up inside. "I don't think it can hurt anything," I said vaguely.

"Really? Even if he's, you know, moved on?"

*Dear God, no!* I screamed inside, my heart curling into a shriveled prune. On the outside, I managed to shrug. If that really turned out to be the case, I would probably run sobbing to the airport. Or melt into a puddle of embarrassed goo right on the spot. Or die.

"Why did you end it all last August, Cora? Why didn't you go with him?"

An involuntary sigh escaped my chest. "You know why," I muttered, not wanting to go through the same conversation we'd had a million trillion times. Especially not in a public place with hundreds of people milling about with nothing better to do than eavesdrop.

"I don't think I do know. Don't tell me what you always tell me. Tell me the truth."

"It is the truth," I insisted. "It got really serious, and I was just scared. And he was going so far away. If he broke up with me, I'd be devastated. If he met someone else—better to have a clean break in the beginning." I stopped short. There were a million reasons in my head. They were mostly things I'd seen in movies or read in books. None of them were the *real* reason.

The *selkie* reason.

"So what's changed?" Rosie asked.

"What's with the third degree? I thought you wanted me to go! 'Live a little,' you said!"

"I do want you to go. But I want to know *why* you're going. What has changed since August? All of a sudden you're willing to fly halfway across the world to see this guy—do you not believe any of those things anymore?"

"Ireland isn't halfway across the world."

"Cora!"

"I … I don't know," I stuttered. "I guess I thought I'd be over him by now. And I'm not."

Rosie paused and stared uncomprehendingly at a muted TV screen playing the news. Her eyebrows were drawn low over eyes, her lips pursed. "If we get there and he's got some girl and you fall to pieces, I'm not going to be the one to clean you up, okay?"

I nodded. *Jesus Christ, what if he did have a girl there? Aidan would have told me, right?* Aidan wouldn't have encouraged me to come if …

The thought of another girl in those strong swimmer arms flipped my stomach like a pancake.

"God!" Rosie groaned. "You and I both know I'll clean you up. Forever and always. Every time." She tapped her pointer finger on my nose in our signature move. "I'll be there when—I mean *if* he's already checked out."

The possibility hurt my chest. "I'm not going to fall to pieces," I assured her. "I just—I know a lot about this situation. I want to go to be there for Aidan."

"The 'situation,' huh? You mean their dad? So you aren't going with your sights set on Rory? This isn't about getting him back, this is about being a friend to Aidan?"

I nodded.

"Bullshit, Cora."

I stared at the ceiling of the plane for a long time that evening. The little "WC" became seared into my brain as it lit up and went out each time someone closed the bathroom door. Our seats weren't next to each other, but the flight wasn't full, and we were able to move to one empty middle row of seats. I was glad to have Rosie for the company, even if she was chattering incessantly about Luke the Extraordinary Frat Boy, but any time I looked at Aidan, heard Aidan, or even got a glimpse of him out of the corner of my eye, my mind started off on a wild tangent, running after Rory.

God, our normal problems—like what major to pick for college or whether or not to call Luke the Extraordinary Frat Boy over the summer—all seemed so frivolous now. So tiny. So unimportant.

Before long Rosie was curled up in the two middle seats, snoring loudly and cocooned in a nest of limp pillows and tiny airplane blankets she'd pilfered from empty seats. But it wasn't the snoring that was keeping me awake—it was what she'd said to me earlier at the airport. It wasn't anything I hadn't considered a hundred times before, but it was different when it was taken out of the confines of my own mind and let loose into the real world where other people could say it, hear it, validate it.

What if Rory didn't love me anymore?

For the thousandth time that year, I went over the last time I'd seen him, looking for every possible instance where I should have acted differently. Every time that I had had a choice and had chosen the one that had led me to where I was now. A strange, strange place I never would have thought I could be.

Jetting across the Atlantic on my way to give my first love a second chance. And to tell him about … *everything*.

Our last night on the jetty appeared before me with too much clarity, so much clarity it hurt my stomach, and my chest constricted. Why I didn't just tell him right there—"so, I think Mrs. O'Leary is your mother and you're a selkie"—I don't know. Every time I considered it, my stomach started roiling and I thought I'd puke. *Why didn't you just tell him?* I could see him, standing in front of me as we swayed slightly while the pier rode the waves. His arms were around me and he was so warm and smelled so familiar. He seemed so real right then as I sat on the plane, I was afraid of it showing on my face.

A gentle groan escaped my throat, and I jolted back to the present, glancing at Aidan to make sure he hadn't noticed.

He had.

"Penny for your thoughts?" he said curiously.

I smiled weakly, poking at the questionable meat among the vestiges of the airplane dinner still on my tray. Rosie's dinner had also been shoved haphazardly onto my tray. The lack of food made my stomach ache now. I was not about to give him my real thoughts just then, but there was plenty else we had to wade through.

"There is one thing I've been wondering," I said softly, glancing down at Rosie between us; her mouth was open in sleep. "Why didn't Mrs. O'Leary leave money to you?" *Or talk about you at all?* In all the time I'd known Mrs. O'Leary, she had never shown preferential treatment to Aidan. Not like she had for Rory. There was a niggling memory of Mr. Hall saying something about it, but I couldn't quite remember what.

The plane was quiet and the lights were out, but reading lights scattered about the place provided enough light for me to see Aidan's face. He looked at his hands, and he suddenly seemed thinner and more tired than ever. "Mr. Hall told me she didn't know who I was," he said softly.

"You mean, she didn't know you were her ..." *Son* was the word I couldn't quite spit out.

He nodded. "For some reason she knew who Rory was, but not

me." Did it hurt him? I wondered. That he'd never been as close to her as Rory had been? As I looked at his face under the glow of a nearby reading lamp, I couldn't help but think the answer was a resounding *yes*. "I wasn't around her much, so I guess she didn't have a chance to recognize me. When I was younger, I was pretty shy. And Mr. O'Leary kind of scared me. He used to bring us to hang out with his friends in the shed on the Ritz property sometimes, but Mrs. O'Leary was never there. It was always just a bunch of men talking about fishing and boats. But I wasn't like Rory—out swimming and talking to the neighbors. I preferred books in the comfort of my own room. And then, in later years, Mrs. O'Leary never left *her* house. I wasn't over there all the time like Rory."

"Mr. Hall didn't know *why* she didn't know who you were? I mean, she knew who Rory was, even if everyone thought she was crazy. I wonder how she knew ..."

Aidan shook his head. A few strands of dark hair fell over his eyes. "Guess that's a question for Seamus."

My heart did a weird twist. That name was one I'd heard most frequently in the feeble voice of Mrs. O'Leary. But it had been a long time since I'd heard her outside of my dreams. "Do you know where to find him?" I asked. "Seamus, I mean."

"I have a name. One of his old fishing partners, a friend I guess. Mr. Hall thinks he may have gone to look him up when he first got back to Ireland. But that was more than ten years ago."

"Well that's a good starting point." The end of my sentence was drowned out by Aidan breaking into a fit of coughing, doubled over in his seat. It was so fierce as to make my eyebrows shoot up and my hand stretched out involuntarily as if I could somehow soothe him.

"Are you okay?" I asked when it subsided.

He nodded. "Irish air gets to me sometimes."

With a nervous chuckle, I pointed out, "I think the only air in here right now is Chicago air."

"Ah, right." He didn't offer further explanation and seemed uncomfortable, so I let it drop.

After a few moments of silence, I finally croaked, "Aidan?" I shifted in the uncomfortable airplane seat. My butt had long since gone numb.

"Hmm?"

"Does … does Rory know we're coming … know *I'm* coming?"

Aidan's cheeks went red. That was answer enough. "He'll be happy, Cora," he finally said, clearly trying to assure himself as much as me.

God, what if he wasn't? *"Why did you leave it like that if you love him?"* Rosie had demanded a million trillion times last autumn.

*"We're too young,"* I had said a zillion times. *"How will I know that it's love—that there's nothing better out there—if I never look?"*

But it wasn't that. Rory was the most amazing person I'd ever met. I felt closer to him in one summer than I did to Rosie in a lifetime of summers. It wasn't that at all. But now, even as I came crawling back to him, I was afraid. Afraid of having my heart broken. And maybe that was one of the reasons I found it so easy to run last summer.

And run I did. Like a scared dog with its tail tucked between its legs. Teenagers were meeting vampires and werewolves all the time in the books I read. They'd meet this terrifying magic and welcome it with open arms. Well that was complete and utter bullshit. In reality, they would run just like I did.

Or so I told myself.

Rory had sent me the first email after I left Oyster Beach. It was full of "miss you" and "not the same without you" and typical Rory jokes. I would often take down and hold *The Selkie Folk*, just a hollowed-out shell now, sitting on the shelf above my desk at home.

*"Promise me that one's for a ticket to Ireland,"* he'd said to me that last day on the pier. The last time I had seen Rory O'Brien. I had pinky promised.

*"There's nothing more binding than a pinky promise,"* he had murmured.

At long last, that was a promise I was going to keep.

# *Gaillimh*
# GALWAY

Y OU LOOK LIKE SHIT."

"Thanks," I muttered, staring at myself in the bathroom mirror at Dublin Airport, Rosie appraising me from the next sink over.

"I'd help you out, but I'm at least two shades tanner than you."

"Thanks, again, for your uplifting observations."

"Sorry," she muttered, going back to her makeup. Rosie, being generally more beauty-conscious than me, had had the foresight to pack her makeup in her carry-on. She had tiny travel-size bottles reserved for just this purpose, and they were spread in front of her now on the wet public bathroom counter, a rainbow of colors.

"Have you ever thought about dyeing your hair a little darker?"

"And starting a lifelong cycle of trying to play keep up with your hair color?"

"Well, it might help that bland brown—"

"Rosario! Not! Helping!"

I turned disgustedly back to my own reflection. My "bland" brown hair was greasy and stringy from travel and my gray sweatpants, which had seemed like a good travel idea at my house, now felt trashy and ugly. My freckles stood sharply in contrast to my pale face, and there were massive bags under my eyes. But that wasn't the worst of it. The worst of it was a big red spot that was threatening to turn into a full-fledged zit right on the end of my nose. I looked awful. And I didn't feel too great, either.

Turning in exasperation back to my best friend, I asked, "Can you at least make it look like my hair was washed in the past week?"

An already lip-glossed smile lit her face. "I thought you'd never ask."

After Rosie gave me a carefully messy bun and even mixed some concealers together to get my face under control, we joined Aidan in the hall outside where he sat with our bags.

"My turn," he said, taking his backpack off and heading for the men's bathroom.

"Don't forget the blush!" Rosie called after him.

Dublin Airport—or "Aerfort Bhaile Átha Cliath" as a huge sign proclaimed—was big and bright and airy, but there weren't a whole lot of people around. We'd waited in a small line for a good twenty minutes to get through border control, the entirety of which Rosie spent making fun of the Irish word "aerfort," but when we reached the front, the immigration officer had done little more than glance at my American passport before waving me through. Rosie's and my luggage had appeared in baggage claim fairly quickly, as Aidan examined the bus times I'd written down in St. Louis—he'd brought only the ratty camo backpack he'd shown up with on my doorstep.

As we waited for Aidan in the bathroom, I pulled my laptop out of my bag and propped it on my knees. I'd spent a good deal of the plane journey—when I wasn't reading or thinking about Rory—trying to compose an email to my parents, explaining where I was. I'd finally decided on vague but honest.

I logged on to the free airport internet—a godsend—and tapped out as quick a message as I could.

*Hey, Mom and Dad!*

Almost immediately, I erased the exclamation point and went with the more mature comma. After all, I was in college now. Pretending to be a mature adult might make them treat me as such.

*Just wanted to let you know that Rosie & I decided to go on a little adventure. The Eisenbergs are walking and feeding Princess. I'll be back in two weeks. Love you!*

Once again, I deleted the exclamation point. But a comma just seemed stuffy, so I went with no punctuation at all.

My finger hovered over the trackpad, the cursor planted firmly on "send." With a deep breath, I sent it before snapping my laptop shut and sliding it back into my backpack.

Suddenly I noticed Rosie was elbow-deep in Aidan's backpack.

"Uh … What in the world are you doing?"

"Trying to find that bus schedule he just had," Rosie explained reasonably.

"Rosie! I have it! He gave it back to me!" I snapped, checking to make sure Aidan wasn't seeing this. "Jesus, you can't just go through his stuff!"

"Fine, don't have a cow. But when I marry him, then you have to butt out, okay?"

"Oh God, *please* stop hitting—"

"What is this?" Rosie pulled her arm out like I asked, but when her hand appeared, it wasn't empty.

My mouth dropped open. She was holding the sealskin.

"I don't know—" I must have spoken too quickly because her eyes were disbelieving, accusatory.

"It looks like … like …" Her nose wrinkled in disgust.

"Shhh, Rosie, put it back."

"Cora, what the hell is this?"

I got up, snatched the skin from her, stuffed it in the backpack, and zipped it up. "I will tell you, okay, but you have got to prepare for some weird shit." I was very close to her face, my nostrils letting out angry puffs of hot air.

"Okay," she said softly, her usual snark and sass evaporating.

I looked from side to side to make sure there was nobody within hearing distance. But there was. A little kid with a shock of blond hair was sitting at the feet of his parents, against the wall just a few feet away, and he was looking straight at me.

"Well, what does it matter, anyway?" I huffed. "He's probably heard worse. So, last summer, we found out who Rory and Aidan's real parents are and … and their mom, who's dead now—or … or not dead, but *gone*—she claims they're all selkies. Which are these half-seal, half-human things. Well, not the dad. But her and Rory and Aidan."

Rosie's face was like a stone carving for the longest second. Then she erupted in such laughter, spittle sprayed across my face.

"Glad I shared with you," I said crossly, wiping my forehead with the sleeve of my t-shirt.

"I'm sorry," she said between gasps for breath. "Sorry for spraying your face. Not sorry for laughing."

Aidan walked up then, a question on his face as he watched Rosie roll around on the airport floor, and saw my cross face. I stood up and shouldered my backpack.

"I just told her you're a selkie," I said, grabbing my suitcase and turning toward the big airport doors. The kid with the blond hair stared up at me with big, round eyes. *He's not laughing,* I thought darkly. *But he's probably going to need a therapist when he grows up.*

Aidan's face must have convinced Rosie, but I didn't stick around to see it. "Wait!" she yelped. "You two can't be serious!"

"You still won't give this up?" Rosie asked for the thousandth time. The bus ride to Galway was about two and a half hours, and my best friend was not coming to any supernatural epiphanies here on this quiet, slightly smelly bus.

"Leave me alone, Rosario," I said.

"No!" she snapped. "You two are in on some cruel joke that you refuse to give up."

"If you don't believe me, why don't *you* give it up?" I suggested. On the other side of me, Aidan was fast asleep, completely indifferent to whether or not Rosie handled this latest revelation with grace.

"Because I'm wondering when the hell my *best friend* was going to tell me that a) she needed to be committed immediately and b) that the trip she'd smuggled me away on was a trip to crazy town."

"*Smuggled?*"

"I will swear in a court of law that it was a kidnap, I promise you! Who are they going to believe? Me, or the girl who thinks *selkies*"—she hissed the word like a hyena—"are real?"

"You didn't have to come!" I groaned. And even though I knew I never would have had the guts to make this move without her, at the moment, a Rosie-shaped hole in this trip was enticing.

"Seriously! When were you going to drop this on me?"

I shrugged. "I didn't really have a plan past 'Get on plane.'"

Rosie groaned. "Too far, Manchester! You have gone too far! Here I thought we were going to have our own little Mary Kate and Ashley Euro trip, and the whole time you were scheming with some weird homeless person"—she gestured at Aidan—"to go on this fantasy adventure you probably read about somewhere in the depths of the internet!"

"Hmm, a couple of hours ago, he was hot and you were making

plans to marry him."

"Shit got weird, Cora! Hot goes out the window when shit gets weird! And shit just got real weird!"

That was an understatement—a first for Drama Queen Rosie.

Once we stood blinking in the Galway bus station, the quaking in my stomach had *nothing* to do with the winding Irish roads or Rosie's pestering. I nervously patted Rosie's work on my hair with shaky fingers as we stepped out into the dark Irish night. It was nearly midnight, and the short, colorful buildings left room for the sky to unfold above us with a magnificent showing of stars. The moon was big and bright, probably only a few days away from being full. Around us people were embracing, and excited Irish-accented chatter proclaimed the reuniting of loved ones. I only hoped my own reunion would be as happy.

"How are we going to find him?" Rosie snapped at Aidan, who was already crossing an empty street. "Do vampires or whatsits have some sort of glow about them we can track?"

There was venom in my eyes as I glared at her.

"What?" she demanded with a shrug. "If you're going to be serious about this shit, then I can be serious about thinking you're certifiably insane."

"I promise we'll talk about it later," I said, exhaustion lacing my voice. "Isn't my word and Aidan's enough?"

"That magic is real? No, sorry. If *Harry Potter* couldn't convince me, then you sure as hell aren't going to. Where's my acceptance letter to Hogwarts, huh?"

"Maybe if you'd read the books, they'd have convinced you. Anyway," I said, turning to Aidan. "How are we going to find Rory?"

"I have his Irish cell number," Aidan said, undaunted by Rosie's doubt, "but he should be at a gig right now."

"A gig?" Rosie repeated.

"He's in a band," Aidan explained. "They have a gig tonight at The King's Head pub."

Rosie waggled her perfectly plucked eyebrows at me. "Your vamp is in a band."

"Rosie! I will find an actual vampire and have it bleed you to death if you do not cut it out with the jokes!"

She sniggered, but I was about to be sick.

*Deep breaths*, I instructed myself. I could face Rory without puking. I could do this. I could look at his gorgeous face that was apparently now in a band and stay the butterflies that would inevitably invade my already war-torn stomach. I could stand my ground. But stand my ground *and* look cute? No way. Look normal? That remained to be seen. At the moment I was feeling entirely too fatigued and smelly.

The little city felt more like a town as Aidan led us expertly down street after street. It was rather quiet, and pub after pub lined the way, some playing music through speakers out onto the sidewalk. The shops were all closed up but there was the occasional dance club with a different sort of music drifting through the doors. We cut across a giant grassy square that Aidan called "Eyre Square," and as soon as we reached the top of it, the air around us began to buzz.

A wide, two-way-street-sized pedestrian walk stretched in front of us, full of people. Loud, happy, shouting, singing people. People on guitars and various instruments were sprinkled in front of the colorful storefronts, just enough room between them to be heard over each other. Obviously drunk boys in skinny pants swayed around the buskers, drowning them out with their own horrible voices. Despite the chill in the air, girls in tiny skirts and four-inch heels limped along, some slipping out of their heels to run after friends. For a country that I'd always considered quiet and quaintly rural, this place was *alive*.

For the briefest of minutes, I forgot to think about Rory O'Brien. I was just a traveler in a foreign place, and it was beautiful and I was enchanted.

"It's awesome," Rosie breathed, watching a busker with a guitar climb up onto one of the short metal poles that lined the street.

Though I didn't have a voice at the moment, I had to agree. The buildings here were old, and none more than four stories tall, leaving the dark night sky free and wide open as the tangle of music reverberated between the buildings. Quaint windows lined the walls above the shops, and seagulls screeched overhead despite the dark.

More than one boy with an Irish accent hit on Rosie. She lapped it up like a kitten does milk, her selkie-induced anger melting away with their attentions.

"This place. Is. Awesome." Rosie's smile lit up as she twirled around and led the way down the street, swaying her hips to the tune of "Lady in Red," which leaked out of an ancient-looking guitar.

As I followed in her wake, the realization that I was too underdressed and especially under-showered to go find Rory at a gig made my stomach feel as though an entire colony of leprechauns was dancing a jig in there. The girls on the street were wearing short, glittery dresses that revealed most of their skin. *I'm wearing sweatpants, for Christ's sake!* At least they were my "good" sweatpants, if there was such a thing.

We reached a fork in the pedestrian road, a sign pointing various ways for various attractions. The name of each destination was printed in gold lettering on a black arrow, tilted to point in the proper direction. But our destination didn't have an arrow. There, on the left, right at the fork, was a big red pub with a huge window display over the door. Some sort of finely dressed mannequin was backed by a dusty white curtain. *The King's Head* was painted in gold over the door.

And there, right below the door, his hands in his pockets, his gaze on the ground, was a gorgeous boy in jeans and a bright blue hoodie.

My breath hitched in my throat and I was sure I was going to faint.

His hair was a little different—shorter—but it was him. The first boy to ever tell me he loved me.

# *Grá ar an Chéad Radharc*
## LOVE AT FIRST SIGHT

I NOTICED HIM BEFORE AIDAN, BUT BEFORE I could alert anyone, another guy poked his head out the front door of the pub and gestured to Rory, who darted inside.

"Here," Aidan said, pointing at the door Rory had just disappeared through. "The King's Head. They're playing here."

I kept my mouth shut and followed him up to a big bouncer who checked our I.D.s before allowing us inside.

"There is some real talent in this room," Rosie breathed, scurrying excitedly after Aidan as he delved deeper into the dark space. "I guess I should have known based on Colin Farrell, but *man*. The Irish have it going on!"

It was loud and decidedly like the Irish-pub-imitation

bars I'd been to in the U.S. *Thank God it's dark*, I thought, tucking an errant strand of bland brown hair behind my ear. Aidan led us over the stone floor, past a huge fireplace, and through a narrow room to the heart of the bar, where the crowd was gathered around a wooden stage. It fit into the corner of the room and opened up to a second floor above.

And there he was.

He was slipping a guitar over his head and talking to the guy in the center of the stage who was adjusting a microphone. That guy had a guitar, too, and there was a bassist and a drummer, as well.

*He plays guitar now.* What else had I missed in this year of self-imposed exile?

As I fell to pieces in the middle of a foreign city, Rosie came to life once more in her natural habitat.

"I'm leeeeegal!" she shrieked, shaking her butt in happiness. "Do you want a drink?" She was practically yelling in my ear as she ditched her giant bags next to the bar, ignoring the weird looks from nearby patrons.

I put a hand to my stomach. "Unless you want me to paint this place the colors of my airplane dinner, I don't think so." She wrinkled her nose. "Never mind," I mumbled. "No thanks."

"Aidan?"

He shook his head, standing on his tip-toes to get a better view of Rory.

Without preamble, the drummer on stage began a count and they erupted into a song I didn't recognize. The singer whined rather well, but it didn't matter. After nine long months, there was no way I could take my eyes off Rory. He played quietly, understated, not thrashing around like the singer was. And he looked like a god.

His short, dark hair was just the tiniest bit messy, and I couldn't help but note that he seemed to be wearing gel, which, based on the crowd in front of me, was probably a practice adopted from the Irish boys. His jeans hugged his hips perfectly, and he'd already shed his hoodie, the black t-shirt remaining sporting a cartoon of Darth Vader playing the guitar. Ireland had decidedly *not* injured his tan, and the muscles in his arms worked gently as he played. He was just like I remembered him. Familiar, beautiful, a welcome sight that put a warm comfort in my stomach while at the same time growing goose bumps on my arms.

The bass and guitars eased then, the drummer keeping time, and the singer started a clap. Rory let his guitar hang from its strap around his shoulder and grabbed something from his back pocket. A tin whistle.

All the air in the room whooshed at me, as if I was caught in my very own emotional tornado.

He embarked on a complicated solo to the emphatic whistling of the crowd, his tennis shoe tapping against the stage floor as he played. I didn't know the tin whistle could rock so hard. His cheeks puffed and deflated in rapid succession, and I suddenly felt humbled. It stilled my heart to know that this boy had chosen *me* last summer. This beautiful guy had held *me* and kissed *me*. He'd wanted *me*. How on earth had I managed to mess that up so magnificently?

Aidan squeezed farther into the throng of people to get closer to the stage and I followed reluctantly. It was that or stand awkwardly by myself in a foreign country.

As the tin whistle solo ended and the rest of the band jumped in, Rosie found us again, this time brandishing two glasses of something that could have been beer. "It's so great to be legal!" she cried, twirling in a messy circle that spilled the cold liquor all over my shoes.

A guy who looked at least thirty grabbed Rosie's arm, his eyebrows quirked in question, as an actual question would have gone unheard.

Rosie squealed and handed her drinks to me before twirling away with him—literally. He spun her and swayed and kicked like I imagined my parents would have at a sock hop. Or a disco. Or whatever era they were cool in. No American-style grinding here, then.

And just as I sniffed Rosie's drink—sweet and acidic—my cheeks lit on fire. Because his eyes met mine.

I froze like a deer in headlights. And so did Rory.

The familiar lips broke open in surprise, and Rory's fingers fumbled on the guitar. His bandmates were too loud for anyone to notice. His glittering dark eyes bore the surprise like a wounded puppy.

*Dear God, I'm gonna be sick.*

Rory tore his gaze away from me and stared at his guitar, his Adam's apple bobbing as he gulped.

I was free to stare all I wanted the rest of the gig because he studiously avoided my eyes. Those gorgeous eyes that had been so close to mine so many times, that had fluttered closed as I kissed them so many times. Those eyes looked at Aidan with a small, amused shake of the head, they looked at the crowd, they looked at the singer, the drummer, even the bartenders. But I was suddenly invisible.

By the time Rory put his guitar down and followed his bandmates off stage, Rosie had danced with at least four different men. And she was far from sober.

"Which one's the vampire again?" she asked for the fifth time.

Neither Aidan nor I had to answer because he was coming toward us. Quickly. He laughed a disbelieving laugh before attacking Aidan with a hug.

"What the hell?"

*Mmm.* That voice. How many times had I imagined that voice? Dreamed of it? Like a game of telephone it had been tweaked and edited by my imagination until it was unlike the original. The memory that hit me upon hearing it again was like a brick to my battered gut.

"Surprise," Aidan said with a chuckle.

"I'm Rosie!" my eloquent friend yelled, shoving in front of Rory.

"Hi," he said. His hand reached out to shake hers, but she suddenly noticed one of her "new friends" as she was calling them and ran off into the crowd.

Rory glanced at me before turning back to Aidan. "Why didn't you tell me you were coming?"

"Because you would have told me not to," Aidan said, as if stating the obvious. Their exchange came to an abrupt end as Aidan glanced at me. Great. I was the elephant in the room. "I, uh, didn't have enough to get here alone, so Cora helped," Aidan explained awkwardly.

"No—I—we used the money from Mrs. O'Leary's books," I

explained quickly. As Rory's eyes fell on me, everything in me grew hot, and I was sure my new pimple was glowing like a red beacon, effectively making me a real-life Rudolph.

"Well, thanks," Rory said uncomfortably. His eyes fell to his yellow and blue tennis shoes as he stepped forward and slid his arms around my shoulders. It was the weakest, most pitiful hug I'd ever been a part of, but the feeling of his skin against mine was enough to bring a prickling feeling to the backs of my eyes.

How had I messed things up with this boy so incredibly, horrifically bad? And how had I ever thought getting on that plane and showing up here would turn out okay?

"Where do Mum and Dad think you are?" Rory asked when he pulled away, speaking to Aidan again. It was as if the mere sight of me was poison to those gorgeous eyes of his. "She would never agree to you borrowing money from a stranger to come here."

*A stranger.* That's exactly what I felt like at that moment.

"I'm in Cleveland visiting Johnny Marsden," Aidan said reasonably.

"That kid you went to middle school with?" Rory asked, confused.

"That 'kid' was one of my best friends!" Aidan said defensively. "We talk. Sometimes."

"That's the best cover you could come up with?" Rory shook his head and moved away from us. We drifted toward the bar in his wake.

"Hey! I even got one of my friends to pretend to be his dad. Mum talked to him on the phone. I really worked on this."

"You know that game won't last long," Rory said with a shake of his head. "And since when do you break the rules?"

"Times are a'changing, brother." The way Aidan was grinning and his eyes were shining, I got the feeling he really meant that.

"What brings you here anyway?" Rory asked.

"We … well … we have a lot to talk about," Aidan said vaguely.

Rory's eyebrows rose. "Such as?"

Aidan glanced at me again. At least *somebody* could stand to look at me. "It's kind of massive," he said, his eyes darting around the room. "It probably shouldn't happen here."

"Are you okay?" Rory asked quickly.

"Yeah, I'm fine!" Aidan assured him. "But, there's just a lot we have to catch you up on." He tipped his head sideways at me.

"Well"—Rory glanced at the chunky silver watch on his wrist—"I guess it'll have to wait until tomorrow, I have to be at work in ten minutes."

"Tonight?" Aidan asked. His face looked crestfallen. In all my excitement to see the first—and only—boy I'd ever loved, I hadn't even realized that maybe Aidan was extremely excited to see his big brother.

"Somebody's gotta take care of the drunken masses," Rory said with a heart-rending grin. As he bent to retrieve a navy blue backpack from behind the bar, it occurred to me just how much this boy's life had changed in the past nine months. He was in a band, and he apparently had a job. Where did he work? It dawned on me just how much I had to learn about him again.

"Here, it's apartment one in the block above O'Flaherty's Chemist. Right by the Oscar Wilde statue." He handed a ring full of keys to

Aidan. "The orange is for the gate, the gray is the building door, and the green is the apartment door."

"Orange, gray, green. Got it."

Rory tugged the blue hoodie out of his backpack. I watched his shoulder muscles—still strong from swimming—stand out as he slipped into the sleeves. "You look exhausted, you should get some sleep. Don't wait up for me, I'm not off 'til five. I'll come back here for my guitar tomorrow. You guys can sleep in any of the bedrooms, my housemates have both gone home for the week." He looked at Aidan for a long moment before enveloping him in another hug. "I'm really glad you're here."

I was sure he was going to leave without another glance at me, but his eyes fell on my face as he walked away and said, "I'll see you later."

I'd dreamed of it a million times—seeing Rory again, talking to him again. *Kissing* him again. But I'd finally traveled all that way and the unthinkable had actually happened.

Rory O'Brien didn't want to see me.

# *Faoistin Thar Áma*
## AN OVERDUE CONFESSION

I COULDN'T VERY WELL GET ON A BUS AND GO BACK to the airport, at least not while Rosie was drunk, so I numbly followed Aidan back to the top of the pedestrian street aptly called "Shop Street."

"That's a stupid name," Rosie had slurred as Aidan explained it.

"If you think that's ridiculous, just wait," Aidan said, obviously amused by Rosie's present state. "Pharmacies are chemists'. Ladybugs are ladybirds. And a shopping cart is a trolley."

"Ridiculous," Rosie muttered, plopping down in the middle of a bench beneath an old-fashioned lamppost. Two slightly larger-than-life statues sat on either end of the bench, facing each other as if conversing, leaving just enough room between them for a drunk like Rosie. A guy with a banjo stood serenading passersby and leaning against the statue on the left, who was apparently supposed to be Oscar Wilde.

"Here we are," Aidan said. He was treating me delicately, and I knew he'd noticed my lukewarm reunion with Rory.

Behind the statues was a pharmacy and tucked above those were three rows of big wooden windows. Around the back of the "chemist" there was a big black gate. I grabbed Rosie's hand to get her away from the busker who had started serenading her with his banjo. Aidan led us up a steep flight of stairs that took Rosie quite a few tries to get up. As Aidan fumbled with the building door and we argued about the order of keys—I really believed in gray, green, orange—a seagull stood in the corner of the courtyard and teased us loudly.

"Yellow! Purple! Blue!" Rosie yelled at the top of her lungs at the seagull.

"Shhh!" I already regretted bringing her along.

"Gray!" Aidan exclaimed triumphantly.

We stumbled up one more flight of stairs, past a hairdresser's, before finding the royal-blue door of apartment one. Inside, a narrow hallway led to a big sitting room where we were accosted by a tiny, football-size terrier.

"Calm your tits!" Rosie roared at the dog, who actually turned and hid under a table in the corner of the room. There was a big TV facing two leather couches, a tiny kitchen tucked in the corner, and the entire front wall was made up of the big wood-lined windows we'd seen from below. It was from underneath a table next to these windows that the dog peered at us now, a growl in his throat.

"That's Rex," Aidan explained with a smile. "One of Rory's roommates has a dog. I … uh … I wouldn't try to pet him or anything just yet."

*Wasn't going to try.*

As Rosie collapsed on one of the leather couches, I deposited my stuff on the ground. As I perched next to her, my finger messing with a huge gash in the leather that revealed the white foam guts of the couch, the weight of the day came tumbling down on top of my shoulders and a few tiny tears escaped the corners of my eyes.

Refusing to let those get the best of me, I stood back up and proceeded to get Rosie set up in a room that appeared to belong to a girl. The plain white walls were plastered with posters of bands I'd never heard of, but the bedspread was covered in roses and the windowsill held three carefully tended potted plants. I stepped over to a shelf in the corner that held a bunch of framed photos.

From most of them, groups of very pretty girls looked out in laughter. My stomach twisted. I flipped off the light and left Rosie in the dark to get away from those smiling faces as quickly as possible. Aidan took the other roommate's bedroom, leaving Rory's open for whenever he finally did get a chance to sleep. I would sleep on the couch.

If I could sleep at all.

After resisting Aidan's attempts to make me take the third bed, he'd given me a pillow and a heavy blanket. But as I lay there, Rex still under the table, a warning rumbling in his throat, I kicked off the heat of the blanket. Rex yelped in surprise.

Great. Now there were two in Ireland who didn't want me here.

Eventually, after Rex's grumbles subsided to doggy snores, I dragged a chair over to the window and looked down onto the main thoroughfare of the city. The apartment was quiet, the huge, thick walls of the old building keeping out the cacophony of amateur musicians, drunk singers, and seagull chatter outside. I nudged open one of the big windows.

"Sweet Caroline" drifted up to me laced with discordant voices. I glanced at the digital clock on the microwave. 2:50 a.m.

Time to form a plan of action. I couldn't hop back on a bus to the airport, running away *again*. At least not without talking to Rory first. I would be asleep before he came home and in the morning, I would undoubtedly wake up long before he did. Then I could shower and hopefully get back some of my courage just by brushing my hair. And then what? What was I supposed to say to him? All the things I'd rehearsed sounded fake to my own ears now.

"You're a selkie, oh, and I love you." My voice cracked and I looked around quickly, realizing I'd spoken out loud. I studied the room several times, suddenly afraid I wasn't alone. But only Rex was there to lift his head in confusion, his ears perked.

"Go back to sleep," I said. At least one of us could get some rest. My stomach was still tumbling and I didn't trust myself to lie down, so I continued to sit by the window. Just after 3 a.m., the streets flooded with people, completely unaware of me up here watching them, and I blushed as a couple started making out against the locked door of a jeweler's shop.

Nobody took any notice of them, as if sucking face in public was an ordinary, accepted part of a night out. And, apparently, it was. A revelation like that should have made me ecstatic with the possibilities of kissing Rory absolutely everywhere in this romantic town. If only tonight hadn't gone like it had.

The splintery wood of the jetty rocked beneath my feet, a familiar feeling that had come, over the months, to spur a queasy feeling in my stomach. I couldn't see anything in the darkness, but I knew it was there. Just out of my sight. If I squinted and waited, it would come …

And it did. The arm floated into view first. Then a leg. The bloated body of Rick Johnson was familiar, but that didn't stop the bile from rising in my throat as the face blurred and took on the form of an entirely different face. A face I knew.

A face that had stared down at me from the mantelpiece for all my life. So familiar, yet the face of a stranger. A small, button nose and wide, brown eyes. A child for eternity. I never knew her. I'd never spoken to her. And I never would. So why did I feel like crying?

Any semblance to Rick Johnson was gone. The dead body in the water was Gretel, my sister.

Before I knew it, the face was changing again. Rory's eyes looked up at me, huge, round, and lifeless.

A terror-filled scream escaped my lungs. Something slimy was on my face, and I bolted upright.

Into the real world.

A trickle of drool was escaping from my lip. My chest heaved, the terror seeping away slowly. Rory had never been in that dream before. Seeing him today must have caused the change. I pulled my bare arm across my mouth.

"You should have taken one of the beds."

*What the—*

My neck snapped around as I jumped in the wooden chair, my head tearing away from the cold window I'd been leaning on. Rory stood in the doorway to the sitting room, his perfect shape framed by a streetlight coming through a window behind him, Rex standing excitedly in front of him, his little body wiggling.

I sucked in a breath. "I'm sorry, I was—I didn't mean to—"

He smiled, the first smile he'd spent on me yet. "You should go to sleep; you must be really tired." He dropped his navy backpack on the floor.

How could I have possibly fallen asleep leaning against the hard, chilled glass of the window? *Damn jet lag.*

I needed to act aloof. Distant. Nonchalant. Normal people didn't fly across an ocean chasing down their first love. At least not normal people outside of romantic comedies. But I wasn't normal. And Rory knew that.

"No, I'm-I'm not," I said, sitting up straight and putting a hand to my mouth to make sure I wasn't still drooling. Because the way he pulled off his hoodie, revealing the tiniest bit of skin at the bottom of his shirt, was indeed drool-inducing.

He pulled another chair over to the glass, sitting at the opposite end of the long bank of windows, and Rex hopped into his lap.

"Thought you'd be in Oyster Beach this time of year," Rory said, stroking the little dog's furry brown ears.

"I—uh, I think my parents are going in July. I probably won't go with them."

His eyes were on the street below, which was empty except for a pair of street cleaners. "You know, you didn't exactly keep in touch. So what brings you here? A vacation?"

Whoa, he was *not* wasting time on niceties. How was I supposed to answer that? I nodded but realized he wasn't looking at me. "I guess so," I croaked.

One of the street cleaners was scraping at an overturned pizza with a long stick. The other was in a miniature truck with a giant brush on the front that swept trash up like a big broom. The back of the truck let out a steady stream of soapy water, creating a shallow river of suds in its wake. From the white foam, a memory swirled into existence and my cheeks reddened.

We'd stood on the jetty and he'd made me promise I'd come to Ireland. I'd said I would—as soon as I could take a vacation. And his face had fallen. He'd repeated the word "vacation" as if I'd just slapped him in the face.

I hadn't understood it at the time, but I did now. That summer, this summer, he thought he was just the vacation to my regular life. And everything I'd done recently seemed to affirm that.

"No!" I said suddenly, loudly.

Rory ripped his gaze from the street to look at me like I was a lunatic. Which, all things considered, I was beginning to become.

"I mean, no, that's not the reason at all."

"Oh?"

*Don't you dare back down, you chicken!* Self-abuse aside, I was feeling relatively confident. "I came because I missed you," I said with as straight a voice as I could muster.

It hung there in the room, a giant question mark begging to be answered in kind. He didn't say anything. But he looked at me and smiled a tentative, almost watery smile that put the tiniest Band-Aid on my heart and convinced me to go on.

"And-and there's some stuff Aidan and I have to talk to you about," I said.

"What stuff?" I could see the confused, almost hurt look in his eyes. The one that said, *What could you and my brother possibly have in common?*

It hit me then what he must be thinking. "I—it's not—I ..." Breathing heavily through my nose, I stared at my thumbs, thoroughly disgusted with my inability to form complete sentences around this boy. It was like I'd just met him all over again. "I think you should wait for Aidan to wake up," I finally said. *Chicken,* I thought.

"Cora."

The sound of my name on his lips was more than I could bear. My gaze traveled up to his face where his eyes seemed to call out with a voice of their own. Pleading with me to tell the truth. To *finally* tell the truth.

"Sorry," I murmured. "I just … everything's not quite clear in my head. Some things don't make sense."

"Okay …" he said, waiting for me to form a rational train of thought to vocalize.

Where could I possibly begin? I had to be rational about this. But seeing the sealskin in Aidan's hands in our guestroom had sent an unrelenting cold creeping through my stomach and it came back to me now as I sat across from Rory. Last summer I'd run all the way back to St. Louis like a scaredy cat, and I'd stayed there, in my fear, all year. Lying to myself, lying to Rory. He didn't deserve that. Just because Mr. Hall had decided to keep this secret from Rory didn't mean I should have, too.

And I wasn't going to anymore.

"Remember those animal skins in Seamus's shed? The ones you boxed up and gave to Mr. Hall?"

"Yeah?" His voice was surprised, confused.

"I think they were … selkie skins. Mrs. O'Leary's. And-and yours and Aidan's."

The silence had a heartbeat of its own. The street cleaners had moved on, leaving the early-morning storefronts as quiet as I'd seen them yet. But in here, the quiet pounded like a life-giving force. If only it could put enough life in me to go on.

"What?" Rory finally said, his eyes narrowed in suspicion of some sordid prank.

A dam inside me burst. "I know—trust me, I *know*, Rory—I know it sounds crazy!" Uh-oh. The rambling that accompanied my nerves was a painful fact of my existence and it was coming on now. "But you just have to listen to this! Remember there were three skins? You said so yourself. One was missing, but there were two in Seamus's shed, remember? And Mrs. O'Leary went back, she finally found hers and went back to…to the sea or whatever. Well, she didn't find it but Mr. Hall finally decided to give it back to her. He's the one that told me all this—us. He told Aidan, too. And Mr. O'Leary was the one that got you guys adopted—he's your real dad. You were actually seals for a while and he…he found you or something and got you adopted by the O'Briens. And he's not dead—he never disappeared. Well, I mean, he did, but not to the sea like everyone thought. He ran away! He ran away here, to Ireland, and left Mrs. O'Leary. Who is—was—I don't know, but she's your mom. You're the babies that disappeared all those years ago. You really are Ronan. And that makes you, well, selkies. Or … half … or something …"

*So much for rational, Cora.*

At least I wasn't invisible anymore. Those dark eyes I'd dreamed about more often than not held my own now, daring me to crack a smile or reveal any sign that I wasn't completely and utterly serious.

The distance between us had never seemed so large. The three huge, sparkling panes of glass stretching between us seemed bigger than the Atlantic. Even Rex was looking at me like I was a psychopath.

"I know it sounds crazy!" I yelped. "But it, I don't know, it all fits. I'm serious. I just, uh"—a nervous chuckle escaped me—"I wish I wasn't."

"Are you aware of how insane that sounds?"

"Of course!" As if jumping on a plane and flying across the world for this confession wasn't enough, it had to be a *crazy* confession, too.

"And you're still going to stick by that story?" He spoke slowly, calmly even. I don't know what I expected. Shouting? Jumping around? Yelling? This was Rory. He didn't have a violent bone in his body. I shouldn't have expected anything less. But this quiet disbelief of his was maddening! I wanted him to tell me I was stupid or should be locked up or *something* to dispel the guilt that it had taken me this long to tell him.

"I'm not sticking by anything, Rory, I'm just telling you what Aidan and I were told!"

"Were you and Aidan having these little discussions with Mr. Hall last summer?"

"Well, he didn't tell Aidan 'til this year, right before he died. He…he had cancer." *Oh, shit*, did he even know that? Had I just broken the news of the death of a neighbor as callously as possible? "He told me last summer, yeah," I added quietly.

"Why would he tell that stuff to *you*?"

I shrugged. Who knew? This world didn't follow any rules of logic any longer.

The muscles in Rory's face worked as his eyebrows drew lower over his eyes, and I could see the way his mind was tossing and turning. Those beautiful eyes turned dark, closing down, boarding up, shutting me out.

"I think you should get some sleep," he finally said.

I wanted to argue, but I was, in fact, getting too tired to form any semblance of an argument. My eyelids felt heavy and every limb pulled me down as if the floor was a giant magnet. I got up silently and took a step toward the couch.

"I'll sleep on the couch," he said, putting a hand out to stop me. "Take my bed."

"No, Rory, I'm fine—"

"Seriously, just take my bed."

"No, you're too tall for the couch—"

"Cora." Once again my name in his glorious voice stopped me short. It floated around and around my head as if coming from a dream. When he was sure he'd won the argument he said, "See you tomorrow."

I walked to the door and in one last burst of confidence said over my shoulder, "I'm really happy to be here." I didn't have the nerve to turn and watch his reaction so I simply waited in the doorway. Would he even respond?

"It's good to see you," he said.

It wasn't exactly the *I still love you* I'd hoped for, but it was better than nothing. Maybe I wouldn't get the first bus back to Dublin Airport … er, *aerfort*, after all.

# *Margadh an Domhnaigh*
# THE SUNDAY MARKET

M Y HEART REGISTERED THE HEAVEN OF RORY'S scent before I even opened my eyes. The smell of lemon and the tiniest bit of musky old building mingled with the familiar scent of his deodorant and cologne. I peeked out over the blankets at the sun falling gloriously over the room I'd only barely noticed last night in my fatigue.

The bed was big and comfy with red- and white-cased pillows and a huge, fluffy comforter bearing the logo of some soccer team. A closet graced one corner and a dresser the other, and the far wall held a bank of windows identical to the one in the sitting room. The sun shined through them now, casting the shapes of the windowpanes onto my covered legs, and I couldn't contain the smile that escaped.

*I just woke up in Rory's bed!*

Sure, it would have been preferable if I hadn't woken up *alone* in it, but, hey, I knew how to celebrate baby steps.

Pulling back the covers, I jumped out of the bed and padded over the gray carpet to the windows, which revealed the busy Sunday morning below. Shoppers squeezed around the people—mostly tourists with cameras—that stood, transfixed, to watch buskers and other street performers and pose with Oscar Wilde. One guy wore a microphone and talked down to the audience as he rode an absurdly tall unicycle.

Their smiles were infectious.

*It's good to see you*, Rory had said. I could work with that.

The apartment was still quiet, but Aidan appeared when he heard my door open.

"Breakfast?" he suggested. "Rory and Rex are still asleep, so I figured we'd let the kitchen rest and go grab something from the weekend market."

"Who the hell punched me last night?" Rosie snapped, appearing in the doorway to the suspiciously girly bedroom.

"Nobody punched you, why?" I asked, reaching to wipe smeared mascara off her cheeks.

"My head sure feels like somebody did."

"Ah, that would be the Bulmer's," Aidan said. "You downed quite a few ciders last night."

"I don't know what that means but will somebody feed me?" Rosie asked helplessly.

"If you put on some clothes first," I said. "That is, clothes that you *weren't* wearing last night." Which is what she was currently in.

Shop Street was even more glorious in the light of day. It was impossible to walk a straight line, dodging strollers and kids of all sizes and people who walked slowly to accommodate ice cream, coffees, and crepes. Not to mention the plethora of dogs—some waiting patiently in front of shops, others tied up to posts to await accompaniment, but most off-leash and traipsing obediently beside their owners. An artist had a long line of colorful canvases leaning against a chemist, and a pair of dreadlocked girls sold teeny tiny kites from boxes hanging around their necks, each guiding an orange and green kite above the heads of the crowd.

Right before the fork in the road where The King's Head was, Aidan steered us down a small alley on the right, formed between the back of the row of the buildings on Shop Street and the front of an old, imposing church.

It grew more crowded as booths lined the back doors to the pubs and shops and the tall black fence that enclosed the old churchyard covered in shaggy grass and crumbling, ancient-looking graves.

"They say Christopher Columbus prayed there before he went off to find the new world," Aidan said, gesturing toward the church. "Sort of unlikely, but …"

"Is it true?" I asked.

"Nooo," Rosie groaned, pointing a shaky finger at a mass of at least twenty kegs that were stacked next to the back door of a pub.

"Hush, you're ruining my grasp of Irish history," I told her. "And if you're going to puke, please face that way." I pointed toward Aidan.

"I'm not going to puke," Rosie said, pushing her oversized hot pink Gucci sunglasses up her nose. "I'll have you know I was on the winning team of the Phi Kap Flip Cup Tournament this year. I can handle anything."

"That's both disgusting and inspiring," Aidan said, moving through the crowded alley.

Each booth was packed with interested buyers being sweet-talked by colorful locals, hawking wares that ranged from sunflowers to chocolate. There were all kinds of flowers, locally grown vegetables, paintings of the different sites around Galway, wood carvings, babies' shoes, tiny trinkets that resembled fairies, handmade jewelry, fresh fruit, beautiful glazed pottery, pesto, olives, coffee, soups, doughnuts—

"Falafel!" Rosie screeched, ripping her sunglasses off her face.

"Ah!" I mock-cringed at her face. "Put 'em back on, for the love of God!"

She shot me a withering look—which was all the more scathing for her bloodshot eyes, but obeyed and scurried off toward a big white truck to buy falafel from a man who looked like a hippie.

Aidan and I lapsed into silence then, but it wasn't an awkward one. We were similar in that we could be in comfortable silence without feeling the need to fill the void. I felt a strange companionship with this boy, to whom I had not spoken more than ten words until forty-eight hours ago.

The street came to a big store that read *Cheesemonger's* with a large concrete area in front of it, forming a triangle of open area with the front of the church and a street, then snaked to the right around the church.

The big black fence of the church broke off to make way for a stretch of crumbling old wall before starting up again on the other side.

"What's that?" I asked. There was a big window-size hole in the wall with a skull and crossbones imprinted in the stone beneath it.

Aidan shrugged.

"Ye've not heard of the Lynches before?" a heavily accented voice behind us brought us both twirling around.

An older man in a sweater vest over a plaid shirt ambled toward us, his hands clasped behind his back. He carried a gnarled cane behind him—that he apparently didn't need for walking—and wore one of those wool flat caps that so many older Irish gentlemen wore.

"Uh, no, we haven't," I said, glancing at Aidan and wondering if I'd just met the Irish male equivalent of Mrs. O'Leary. *Which would make him ... Mr. O'Leary?*

"Martin Freeley," he said, with a tip of his cap.

*Damnit.* Well, I couldn't expect it to be *that* easy, could I?

"That very window is the site of a gruesome death," the old man went on. "The very death that coined the term *lynch*. You see, it was a Mayor Lynch back in the fifteenth century that had a rogue of a son. He killed a Spaniard for carousing with his lady. Or so they say."

"And this is where he killed him?" I asked, jabbing my thumb over my shoulder at the wall.

"Oh, no," Martin went on, a disturbing twinkle in his eye. "What happened here was his punishment. His father, as mayor of the city and a fair man, had to condemn his son to death. After all, he was as a murderer."

A chill skittered along my spine despite the warmth of the day.

"They say the crowd was so thick, they couldn't get through to the execution site. So Mayor Lynch tied a rope around his lad's neck and launched him from this very window."

He waited for the effect of his words. I glanced at Aidan, who looked horrified. The sight of his coffee-colored eyes reminded me of another parent I knew who was once accused of killing her own children.

"Or so they say," Martin added, twirling his cane in front of him and continuing to amble down the street, melting seamlessly into the market crowd.

Aidan and I simultaneously turned to face the window which suddenly seemed less old and crumbly and more threatening.

"I feel like lynching you both at the moment."

"Ah!" Aidan and I jumped, whipping around once again, our arms smacking into each other in the process.

"Jesus, Rory! You scared the shit out of us!"

Rory looked at his brother like he was sprouting wings. "Okay," he said in a sing-song voice. "Let's move on and talk about another scary topic."

My cheeks blushed. "I told him everything," I said quietly, tucking the little hairs that strayed from my ponytail behind my ears. I *really* needed to shower if I was ever going to feel confident looking Rory in the face again.

Aidan glanced at me sharply before looking back at his brother, his eyebrows raised. "Well?"

"Well what?" Rory snapped. "I figured out she was insane last night"—he jabbed a finger at me—"but now I can tell you're riding the same crazy train."

"Falafel?" Rosie appeared, holding her falafel in my face, then Rory's and Aidan's.

"No thanks, I've lost my appetite," Rory said, staring between me and Aidan. "Probably for the next century."

"I don't care what either of you believe right now," Aidan said. "Once we find Mr. O'Leary, he'll be able to explain everything."

"So you don't think he died at sea ten years ago like everyone else in the world thinks?" Rory demanded.

I knew, for a fact, even *Rory* didn't believe that. He'd told me so the night we'd spent together in a cabin at O'Brien Resort, which of course brought to mind sweet memories of my cheek pressed against his chest as I fell asleep to the sound of his tin whistle. But I wasn't about to open my mouth now.

"He didn't disappear, he's here, in Ireland," Aidan shot back. "I'd put money on it."

"It just doesn't make sense," Rory said, changing tack. "They were, like, sixty when we were born!"

"Mmm, that's very true," Rosie said between bites of falafel.

"Stay out of it, you don't know *anything*," I snapped at her.

"Not if we were actually born fifty years ago and spent half our lives as seals and only came back to our human bodies a couple decades ago. Not if we're really as old as Mr. and Mrs. O'Brien," Aidan countered proudly, folding his arms over his puffed out chest.

"*Mr. and Mrs.* O'Brien?" Rory shouted, incredulous. "They are *Mum* and *Dad.* What is wrong with you?"

"Look," Aidan said, leaning into us and glancing surreptitiously around. "Mr. Hall told me everything. Once we were in seal form, our human bodies didn't age until we were back out. Don't you get it? I'm not eighteen. You're not nineteen."

Rory scoffed.

I blushed, scared to contradict Rory when our relationship was still on such tender footing. But this wouldn't go anywhere unless he believed. "Actually," I murmured, "Mrs. O'Leary told me something about that, too. How when you—" Rory's eyes widened to glare at me. "Sorry, when *they* switch to seal form, their human body doesn't age. When they get back out of the water they're the same age as the day they got in."

All I could imagine was Rory and Aidan in a classic car with slicked, parted hair, all *Mad Men* style.

"What are you saying? That we were seals for thirty years?" Rory clamped his arms over his chest, which was heaving in a way that made my knees wobble.

"Exactly," Aidan said. "Mr. Hall said, when we were babies, Mrs. O'Leary tried to send us back. That's why everyone thought she'd killed them. I mean … us. But really, she just sent us, you know, to the water. Back … back where she came from. And somehow, decades later, Mr. O'Leary got us back. Brought us back, then got us adopted. I don't know how it all worked out, that's why we need to find this guy Mr.

Hall told me about. He might have the third sealskin or he might know where Seamus is."

Rory rolled his eyes. "I wish you were in Cleveland."

"Seriously!" Aidan said, louder this time. "We need to talk to somebody else who was there back then. Mr. Hall told me a lot of stuff, but not all of it made sense. He was really sick, and sometimes he wasn't making very much sense at the end."

"Oh really? Mr. Hall wasn't making much sense as he was telling you you're a magical creature that lives only in myth and legend? Imagine that!" Rory looked at Rosie, as if to say, *See? He is certifiably insane!*

"Hallelujah," Rosie said, mouth full. "I'm with this guy." She jabbed a thumb at Rory.

"Why aren't you listening to me?" Aidan demanded of Rory, crossing his arms over his chest.

"I am! You're saying Mr. O'Leary is our father." Rory licked his lips, his tennis shoe tapping angrily.

"Yes," Aidan replied.

"And Mrs. O'Leary is our mother."

"Yes," Aidan said.

"And you're a selkie."

"Yes," Aidan said, starting to get suspicious.

"And I'm a selkie."

"Yes!"

"Do you hear yourself?" Rory bellowed.

"Okay, okay," I hissed. "As much as I'm enjoying this little exchange, maybe we shouldn't do this here."

"I agree," Rosie said. Pigeons were gathering behind her feet as lettuce from her falafel wrap littered the ground. But the boys ignored us.

"You're not going to find him," Rory said sternly.

"Mr. Hall gave me a name. Colm Vesey, out in Connemara. He might know where to find Seamus."

"What about our parents?" Rory demanded. "The ones who raised us?"

"Mr. Hall said all they know is the same story the whole town heard. That a young, local woman had us but couldn't care for us and wanted to be kept anonymous."

Rory shook his head and opened his mouth to say something, but just then the heavens opened up and a sharp rain began to fall.

"Are you kidding me?" Aidan cried to the sky. No kidding. As if I could look any more bedraggled than I already did.

"Yeeeek!" Rosie shrieked, just now noticing the pigeons at her feet.

People had started to quicken their paces, a few kids running to get out of the rain, and some tourists pulled out umbrellas. But for the most part, the Irish went on, unimpeded.

Aidan, however, selkie or not, was still American. "Shit, let's go back to the apartment!" he said, screwing his eyes up against the rain and dashing off.

"Ahhhh!" Rosie ran after him, dodging the pigeons and throwing the remains of her falafel at them as an offering.

The sun still shone down, flanked by a few off-white clouds, as if the sky itself was unsure whether to rain or shine. "How is this possible?" I cried, joining Rory to follow after the others. "It's still sunny!"

"Welcome to Ireland!" Rory said. "It's beautiful and supremely irritating in a way only Ireland can be!" He grabbed my hand and pulled me toward him to avoid running straight into an off-leash dog. His hand was warm and, at this point, wet, but it made me shiver nonetheless.

It was fleeting—he let go of my hand once the danger was gone. But it was enough to make this dash through the rain a wonderful moment.

# *Ceacht Náire*
## A LESSON IN MODESTY

T HE SEAWATER-GREEN TILES WERE COLD ON MY feet as I turned the knob on the shower.

Nothing happened.

There was another knob above it, smaller and marked only with two words, "light" and "heavy." I tried that one, flipping it back and forth between the two settings.

Nothing.

Panic started to rise in my gut. My dirty clothes—really dirty—lay in a heap on the floor, and my clean clothes were folded neatly on the closed toilet lid. The big black towel Aidan had procured for me hung from a hook on the back of the door. I didn't have a lot of options here.

I fruitlessly searched the shower for more knobs or buttons before turning back to the first. I tried pushing it, pulling, turning, elbowing it, cursing at it.

Nothing.

After a solid ten minutes of my most dedicated critical thinking, I gave up. Wrapping the big towel around me, which thankfully hung nearly to my knees, I peeked out the door.

The warm corridor was empty and the door to the sitting room at the end was closed. I tiptoed down the hall and went right, for the bedrooms.

"Rosie?" I hissed.

The room she'd slept in was empty.

*That's okay,* I'd just peek into the sitting room, get Rosie, and run away as fast as possible.

I took a deep breath and pushed open the sitting room door. "Rosie?" I squeaked, shoving my head into the room.

The door fell all the way open of its own accord. Rory sat alone on one of the couches, his face in his hand and Rex in his lap as a rerun of *The Simpsons* played to the quiet room. Surprise flooded his face and his eyes flew over my body before quickly retreating to my face.

"Cora! Do you need something?" He jumped up nervously. Rex groaned.

*Shit shit shit.*

"Uh, is Rosie around?" It wasn't that big an apartment, I could tell she wasn't.

"Oh, no, uh, she and Aidan ran to pick up some pizzas for us, for … for dinner. And I think maybe something for her hangover." He was standing just a few feet in front of me now and I was sure every inch of my exposed skin was the color of a three-alarm fire.

"Ah," I said helplessly.

Late afternoon sun slanted through the windows, backlighting him like an angel. Soft shadows danced on the walls. "Can I help you with something?" he asked, gulping visibly, as one hand went to anxiously rub his head.

"I, uh …" The admission was humiliating. "Can't get the shower to turn on."

He let out a nervous laugh. "Oh! Of course. Yeah, it's tricky, let me show you."

I padded after him into the bathroom, watching the muscles in his back stand out against his t-shirt—this one had a picture of Mario getting a speeding ticket on the front.

As he moved toward the shower, I surged forward to hide my underwear and bra from view. Because, you know, boys aren't aware that girls wear bras and everything.

"Here, you have to pull this first to turn it on," Rory said, reaching for a string that fell from a small box on the ceiling in the corner of the room.

"Oh," I said. "Wasn't expecting that."

He pulled the string with a *click* and a tiny square on the box above it turned red. "Then you have to turn it on here." He reached for one of the knobs on the shower, and I leaned forward to see which one. To make sure we could avoid my traipsing around in a towel the next time I needed to shower.

But he was just a bit taller than me and by the time I could see over his shoulder, water was springing to life, and he wheeled around to retreat, knocking straight into me.

"Whoa, sorry," he mumbled, grabbing me by my bare arms to steady me.

I was plenty steady, but his arms didn't move from their delicious spots. Suddenly the fluffy gray rug beneath my feet felt like a cloud, cloud eight or nine or whichever one it is that feels like pure heaven.

We stood like that for an eternity, the water thrumming a steady rhythm on the shower and me clutching the knot where the towel was tucked into itself on my chest. His eyes were chocolatey and warm and for the first time since I'd arrived in Ireland, they looked like they were feeling those same emotions they'd felt last summer. Back when he'd loved me.

One of his hands lifted and hovered near my shoulder for the briefest of moments, igniting goose bumps along my arms and legs, and I was sure he was going to touch my cheek. And then …

This was it. Rory was going to kiss me.

*He doesn't hate me after all!* I willed myself to breathe, because if I passed out *before* he kissed me, I would never forgive myself. I wondered if his shorter hair would feel the same beneath my fingers.

A loud sound sent us both reeling backwards. His heel hit the edge of the shower with a painful *thump* and he shuffled awkwardly to the side.

*Boom bada boom.* It took me the longest moment to recognize the familiar ringtone of my phone coming from the heap of jeans on the floor.

I cleared my throat. "Sorry, that's just my—"

"Yeah, so there you go. The shower's good to go now." He moved quickly around me, careful not to touch me, which was quite a feat in this tiny bathroom.

I gave myself an agonizing moment to steady my breathing before digging my phone out of the pocket of my jeans. It was too late and the screen flashed a missed call from "Dad."

*Oh God.* Putting *that* conversation off as long as possible would be best for everyone involved. I'd call him back later. Or maybe email.

But just then the drum tone started again.

*Shit.* Two calls in a row was no laughing matter.

"Hello?" I said, trying to sound chipper. I hadn't expected an interest in my whereabouts or a check-up *this* quickly. And especially not from my father.

"Where the hell are you?" was the loving greeting on the other end.

*Huh.* Apparently I'd seriously misjudged my dad's interest in my summer. They wouldn't even have been back from Los Angeles yet. *Maybe that email was a bad idea.*

The thunder of the shower eased as I turned it off. "Hi, Dad," I said as brightly as I could manage, my voice echoing slightly in the tiled room.

"Let me rephrase that. Why the hell are you in Ireland, Cora?"

I needed to lie. I'd seen enough movies to know this was the point where I needed to lie. "I—" Luckily he was too angry to let me continue, because I had *no* idea where that was going.

"A thousand dollars? You just dropped a thousand dollars at the slightest whim?"

*Whoa.* Something was going incredibly wrong here. My Dad …
lecturing about money? In the entirety of my existence that had never
happened. Not one single *word* of a single *sentence* had ever touched
upon the topic.

"I-I'm … sorry. I have the money to pay you back, I promise. I just
had to use the credit card to book it online and …" I was decidedly bad
at this.

After a heavy pause, his voice went on. "You just can't do things
like that, Cora!" He sounded less angry, more … exasperated. It sent a
strange quiver through me.

There was a loud rush of air into the phone, like he'd just released
all of his soul through a sigh. I had no idea what to say.

"Just, just don't do it again. And don't go changing the return flight
to France or something. I'll see you in two weeks. Try not to spend
much on the credit card."

Not a word about where I was staying, what I was doing, who I
was seeing. Just lamenting the loss of a stack of bucks the size of what
my mom regularly spent on pantsuits at the mall.

Something was seriously wrong.

# *An Ghaeltacht*
# THE GAELTACHT

W E GOT UP VERY EARLY THE NEXT MORNING IN order to get the bus out to Connemara and back before Rory had to work in the evening.

Aidan had spent all yesterday evening looking up all the Seamus O'Learys in Ireland while Rosie, Rory, and I munched on leftover pizza and watched *Friends* reruns. Aidan found a handful of Seamus O'Learys over the age of thirty—thank God for open profiles on Facebook—but they were quickly debunked with the help of Google. Not even a mention of a Seamus O'Leary in Doolin, where Mrs. O'Leary had once told me Seamus was born. But Aidan had more luck with Colm Veseys. Luckily, it was a small country, and even more fortunate—Vesey wasn't all that common a last name. There were two Veseys in the west of County Galway, in the area known as Connemara, but only one of them was named Colm.

The roads out of Galway city were winding and I was afraid of losing the cold pizza I'd had for breakfast.

"And he yelled at you for using too much money?" Rosie asked. I'd just finished telling her about the strange call from my dad.

"Yeah. It was bizarre."

"I don't think I've ever heard my dad say the word 'money,'" Rosie said.

"I know." We lapsed into silence and I found myself staring at the back of Rory's head. He'd been awkward since our almost-kiss, at times even cold, and the tension was unbearable. He'd ignored me almost all morning, and now he was bickering with Aidan in the seat in front of me.

"Thanks for doing this, okay?" Aidan was whispering at his brother. "Is that what you want to hear?

"Yes."

"God, you know I crack under pressure. Just, just play it cool. I owe you big time, I know. Don't tell her—"

"Shh!" Rory hissed, and a beat later, in a completely different voice, he said, "Hey, Mum. Yeah, it's been forever, I know." There was a pause. "Yeah, so, listen, I'm actually calling because Aidan has something he needs to tell you."

I heard the *thwack* of one brother hitting the other.

"You ass!"

"Take it!"

"No, you said you'd—"

"This is just making it worse!"

"Hey, Mum," Aidan finally said, his voice feigning calm. "Yeah, I'm with Rory. That must be a surprise. Uh-huh. Actually, he bought me a ticket for my birthday. I'm sorry I didn't tell you. I didn't think you and Dad would let me go alone." I could hear harsh talking on the other end of the line and marveled for a moment at the wonders of technology. A telling off from across the sea. Much like my own unexpected one yesterday. "Well, yes, it was very wrong of me to lie. But I just wanted some time with my brother, you know? Besides, it was all his idea."

Another *thwack*.

"Yes, I'll be sure to see Conor and Declan and everyone." Pause. "I'm sorry, Mum, I just really wanted to spend some time with Rory. I miss him, you know?"

Man, he was really pulling the heartstrings like a master puppeteer. But it seemed to be working. There was no more hitting.

"My return ticket is in a couple weeks. Since I'll probably be grounded for the next century when I get home, I'll probably stay 'til then. ... Okay. ... Love you, too, Mum."

By the time the bus was stopped by a sheep in the middle of the road with a pair of mini-me's trailing behind her, Aidan had gotten off scot-free. Or at least with a delayed punishment. The sheep family stood in the middle of the road for a good three minutes, holding up our bus to the delight of all the tourists aboard. I myself may have snapped a few pictures on my phone, though I wouldn't admit it to anyone later.

For the last several miles on the bus, giant, yellow-green mountains rose up around us, littered with rocks and sheep and tufts of brown grass and clusters of yellow flowers. It was beautiful, but in a starkly arid way. Almost like a beautiful death was coating the countryside.

"Well, that was … interesting," I said, as we clamored off the bus at Maam Cross, where most of the tourists were also getting off. Rory had explained that this area was called "The Gaeltacht," which meant an area where Irish was still the predominant language, making it a prime tourist hotspot.

Rosie, on the other hand, couldn't see the appeal. "Is this supposed to be a town?" she asked, flipping her giant Gucci sunglasses onto her head. "It's literally an intersection."

"He lives near here," Aidan explained as we regrouped on the side of the road, away from the tourists, next to a big white sign that said *Maam Cross* in tiny letters under the giant words *An Teach Dóite*. "We'll get a taxi from here."

"They have taxis here? It doesn't even look like they have running water."

"Do you know what I've been wondering?" I chirped to drown out Rosie's insult.

"Watch it!" Rory shouted as I stepped backward toward a clump of the yellow-flowered bushes that littered the landscape. "That's gorse, it's prickly."

"Thanks." I smiled as he released my arm, our first touch since our almost-kiss last night. *My botanist knight in shining armor.*

"What have you been wondering?" Rosie asked loudly, cutting

through our romantic moment with an annoyed expression. Subtlety wasn't her style. Surely a lecture from her on the importance of making the first move on a guy was in my near future.

"I was wondering what his real name is," I said, pointing to Aidan who stood a few steps away on the phone. "We know your name is Ronan ..."

Rory looked at the ground, his expression unreadable.

"But I wonder what his was," I finished quietly.

"Ronan. That's a cool name," Rosie mused, stifling a yawn. A taxi appeared before us, or so I assumed. It looked like any other car. The only hint that this guy was actually a cab driver was his picture taped on the windshield next to what appeared to be some sort of certification.

"We're going here." Aidan passed a slip of paper bearing an address to the driver.

"Colm Vesey's?"

"Uh, how'd you know that?" Aidan asked skeptically.

"It's not New York, lad," the man said with a chuckle. "What could a bunch of Yanks want with Colm?"

Rory and Aidan exchanged looks. We'd opted not to call ahead, just in case the man didn't want to see us. Better to sneak attack, that way the only risk was his not being home. We could always come back, but he could hide if he knew we were coming.

"We're relatives," Rory said. Unconvincingly, if you asked me. "Distant ... relatives."

"Oh yeah? I've got a cousin in Boston."

"I'm sure we know him," Rosie muttered.

Our destination was at the end of a short path that was separated from the road by a trickling stream, spanned by a small arched stone bridge. As we got out of the taxi and Rory paid the driver in colorful euro notes, I noticed the house backed up to a lake. A pair of white rowboats tied to wooden posts in the shallow water became visible as we crossed the tiny bridge.

The house itself was a little squat white thing with a door, a window on the right, two windows on the left, and a single chimney. It didn't have a thatched roof, but it might as well have.

Aidan was already at the wooden front door, fist lifted to knock. He nodded for us to join him, the excitement on his face reflected back in the sunny day.

Rory and Rosie spoke at the same time that Aidan knocked.

"Do you even know what you're going to say?" Rory asked.

"Wait, so we think this guy is your dad, right?" Rosie asked.

Both questions were fruitless because Aidan ignored them, holding his ear close to the door.

Nothing happened.

"This isn't their dad, he's their dad's friend," I whispered to Rosie.

"Oh," her face fell. "That's less exciting." She pulled the elastic out of her auburn hair and smoothed it out, reforming the ponytail before putting the elastic back on to hold it in place. Her hair glimmered in the sunlight and I wondered fleetingly what Rory thought of Rosie. Most boys thought she was pretty. Did he? But thoughts like that would get me nowhere. The moment Rory and I had shared in the bathroom was enough to bolster my confidence and I patted my own dull brown hair, hoping it, too, glimmered just a bit in the sun.

"Well, do we call it a day?" Rory asked.

Still nothing had happened and after each round of knocks, Aidan looked less and less excited, his shoulders slumping by a fraction each time.

"I'll call the taxi back," Rory said. As he dug his phone out of his pocket, Rosie and I turned to walk back toward the road. Aidan, ever the optimist, knocked again behind us.

"It is pretty, isn't it?" I said absently. "Barren, but pretty."

"It's pretty," Rosie agreed, "but it's also really creepy. Eerie. Too quiet for how big and open everything is."

"Cé tá ansin?"

The unfamiliar words caused Rosie, Rory, and I all to spin around.

The front door opened to reveal an old man with snow-white hair standing in the doorway, suspenders hooked over his shoulders and attached to dark brown slacks. A grimy old dish towel, dirty gray in contrast to his impressively white button-down shirt, was slapped over his shoulder.

"Can I help ye?" he said in a thick accent after none of us mustered up the courage to speak.

"Hi, uh, Mr. Vesey?" Aidan asked.

"Indeed." The man nodded, suspicion creating a frown on his face. It was old and weathered, wrinkles masking his forehead.

"We, uh, we wanted to talk to you about Seamus O'Leary."

Colm's face cleared immediately, his eyebrows falling back to a look of stupefaction. "Oh. Please, come in."

# *Iascaireacht Imithe Mícheart*
## A FISHING TRIP GONE WRONG

A S I STEPPED THROUGH THE DOORWAY, I couldn't help but notice how thick the wall was. Nearly a foot, at least. This place had to be seriously old. It was dark and cramped, and Colm Vesey had to bend his head to duck into the sitting room. He motioned for us to follow and take a seat on a pair of dusty-looking couches. I perched on the edge of the red couch next to Rosie, who had fallen silent here, so out of her element. This was definitely not a house Gucci had been in before.

A lamp flickered to life in a corner, casting us all in an unearthly glow. There was no overhead lighting, but the bright day outside cast two big rectangles of light onto the floor. I had to screw up my eyes to look at Mr. Vesey where he sat in front of a window.

"Is Seamus alright?"

I nearly jumped out of my skin as something stretched on the floor in the corner. It was an old border collie who came walking toward us, but sat down at Mr. Vesey's feet. She surveyed us through sleepy eyes, clearly uninterested in visitors.

"We, uh, we don't know," Aidan said, taking the reins. "We were hoping you could tell us."

"I haven't seen Seamus O'Leary in nearly … oh, I don't know … five years at least."

Aidan's face fell and I may have imagined it, but Rory looked crestfallen, too.

"The last I heard from him, he was living in Galway, working for a boat company that did tours on the Corrib River," Mr. Vesey said. Well, that was something. "But I'm fairly sure he wouldn't have lasted long at that."

Whatever the heck that meant.

"Thank you, Mr. Vesey," Aidan said, looking around at us for some sort of guidance. I lifted my shoulders helplessly.

"Please, call me Colm. Why are you trying to find him?" He steadily petted his old dog on the head.

*Just tell him*, I thought, since there was no way I was actually going to join this conversation.

"We, uh," Aidan cut a glance at his brother who was staring at his own hands, "we're his sons."

The transformation in Colm's face was startling. His eyebrows fell back even more and his mouth dropped open to reveal a set of brown, crooked teeth, a look of utter horror on his face.

"You what?" he breathed.

"I'm Aidan O'Brien, this is my brother Rory. And we, uh, we've been led to believe that Seamus was our father."

"Our dear Lord, save our souls." A bird flew by the window outside, throwing a fleeting shadow across Colm's face. "Dear Lord almighty. I've seen ye lads before. I was a fisherman in Oyster Beach for many years."

I looked for any recognition on the boys' faces, but neither seemed to recognize the man.

"You … you knew Lia I guess, too?" Rory spoke up for the first time.

The old man shook his head as he said, "Oh, yes. I knew Lia. Is she well?"

Aidan and Rory exchanged glances, then Aidan said, "No. She … she died. Last summer."

"I'm very sorry to hear that." And he looked it. He looked startlingly sad, actually. "I knew Lia and Seamus very well. In fact," he gulped and seemed to struggle with his breathing for a moment, "I was with Seamus the night of the Great Storm."

My quizzical look went unnoticed as Rory and Aidan swapped nervous looks. "Yeah?" Aidan said. "What … uh, what happened the night of the Great Storm?"

"The O'Briens had already adopted the oldest boy."

"That's me," Rory said.

"Yes." Colm's eyes flew back and forth between Rory and Aidan. "And the other …" Colm trailed off.

"What happened that night?" Aidan pressed.

Colm drew in a deep breath and looked at the back of his old dog's head as if the entire story was written there. "Have you ever heard of selkies?" he finally said.

"Yeah, yeah, we know!" All heads swiveled to Rosie. "What?" she said with a shrug. "They're selkies, we got it. Let's get to the good stuff."

I gave Rosie my most incredulous and admonishing look because I couldn't bring myself to actually form words at the moment.

"What?" she said again. "No point wasting time we could be spending in the pub!"

To my surprise and massive relief, Colm let out a long chuckle. But it sounded sad and laced with unreleased tears. When it subsided he said, "I don't have all the answers. But I know what I saw that night. And I think that's why I haven't seen Seamus in years. It drove a wedge between us in the end. How can a secret like that not?"

My blood ran cold. I knew all too well how a secret could wedge itself into a friendship. Or a relationship. Especially your first relationship. Your first *love*.

Involuntarily, my eyes found him. He looked like he was going to puke all over the red and yellow wool carpet in front of him. Aidan, on the other hand, was positively beaming, all his suspicions finally being confirmed by another human being, and a presumably worthy source at that.

"I can't tell you how it happened or why, but I can tell you what I saw. And perhaps you can forgive me by the end of it." His watery eyes looked back and forth between the boys.

"Forgive you?" Rory repeated, just as Aidan said, "Of course," squirming in his seat, dying for the man to go on.

"You've heard of the Great Storm, no doubt," Colm went on. Rory and Aidan nodded. "I was out fishing with Seamus and Kieran Browne and James Cassidy at the time. We were making a good haul, but we were … well, the weather was getting worse. Seamus was ever the logical one, he must have suggested we go back, I don't know, ten times. But we …" Here he stumbled, as if the words were causing him pain. "We … well, the animals must have known a storm was coming because they were moving a lot that day. Long before the bad weather started up. So we'd been …" Somewhere in the depths of the house a clock ticked in the silence until the man finally whispered, "No, I must be honest with you."

I exchanged a confused look with Rory. We waited.

And waited.

Colm took a deep breath and looked at each of the boys in turn before speaking so softly we all had to lean forward to hear. "We'd been hunting seals," he whispered.

I felt cold all over. If Rory and Aidan had been seals at the time, they could've been … but no, Rory had already been adopted. I didn't have time to untangle my thoughts, because Colm was going on resolutely.

"It was a clear, clear day when we started out. There was a great number of young seals that time of year, and they fetched far more at the right market than the few bass or bluefin tuna we found. Seamus would never join the hunting. He thought we were going fishing, but then when we started … Anyway, after we started hunting, that's … *that's* when the storm started. And it seemed as though … the more we killed, the worse the storm got. Mother Nature was punishing us, no doubt." He laughed a bitter laugh, and I could see his eyes were close to spilling his emotions down his weathered cheeks.

"We'd gotten, I don't know … maybe six, when Seamus broke down. He was begging us to go home, but there was this one. This one little seal that was following the boat. It seemed so strange, the boat was downright bloody, but this little seal didn't seem to understand the threat. Seamus just broke down. He was yelling at the animal, 'Get away! Leave! Go away!' We sat him down, thinking he was having a breakdown. Maybe because of his fear of the storm. So we decided to turn back, but James went to make one last kill. The little seal following the boat.

"Seamus tackled him, and James fell overboard. Even the strongest swimmer would have been gone in those waves in an instant."

Silence coated the room as the reality played out in each of our minds.

*Seamus O'Leary had killed a man.*

"It was all over in an instant," the old man whispered.

It was quiet for so long I was sure he didn't have anything else to say. But then the tired dog at his feet padded forward until she was lying on the ground and the movement wakened Colm out of whatever far corner of his past he was buried in.

"I don't know how, but the little seal was in the boat. And then…"

He laughed but it turned into a choke and tears escaped the corners of his eyes. "And then Seamus snatched it up, and there was suddenly a little baby lying in his arms." The tears flowed unchecked as he shook his head in disbelief, even all these years later. "The seal was gone and there was a wee infant. It didn't even cry. It was wrapped up in this, this animal skin. Seamus just held it, like it was the most natural thing in the world."

"That was me," Aidan breathed.

"But Seamus went mad, then," Colm went on. "He screamed at us, threatened us, threatened our families, made us promise never to reveal what we'd seen that day. He said the baby would be adopted by the O'Brien family, but that we could never say a word to refute the story he'd give. That we could never so much as look at the boy askance.

"I couldn't stay there. Especially when Seamus reported James had fallen overboard in the storm. Kieran Browne and I—we both decided we couldn't live in that town. We left the next day. Seamus made me take the … the thing the child had been wrapped in. The skin. The sealskin. Here, to Ireland. Seamus followed, what, six? Seven years later?"

"Do you have it?" Aidan whispered. "Is it here?"

"What?" Colm asked, looking thoroughly confused, as if he'd woken up from a dream and found himself with four strangers.

"The skin."

"Oh." Colm shook his head. "I couldn't live with it. That night haunted me for many years. James still visits my dreams, you know. I've never even gone back to the water. Not the ocean, anyway."

I remembered the lake out back behind the house. His consolation prize. His replacement for the ocean where unfathomable fear now lay for him. I could relate.

"Do you know where the sealskin is now?" Aidan asked.

Colm shook his head, but gave no other answer.

"What did you do with it? Did you give it back to Seamus?"

The old man shook his head. "I threw it out."

Aidan's face fell as he stared at the old man for a long moment. Finally he asked, "Do you know what boat company Seamus was working for in Galway?" His voice was becoming increasingly desperate.

"No, lad, I don't," Colm said apologetically.

"What *do* you know?" Aidan snapped. "What about—"

Who knows what Aidan was about to ask, but Rory put his hand on his brother's shoulder to stop the torrent of questions and insolence. Aidan's mouth became a thin, angry line.

I shifted uncomfortably. This was our only lead. If Colm didn't know anything else, the shoddy investigation we'd pieced together would probably end here.

"Listen," Colm said in his scratchy voice. "I can't tell you where your da is, but I can tell you this: I don't think he wants to be found."

# *Deartháir agus Cac Éan*
## A BROTHER AND BIRD SHIT

THE APARTMENT WAS STICKY HOT, SO THE windows in the sitting room were pushed open, letting in the cacophony of a Galway morning without the fear of mosquitoes. I wondered what it would be like to live without fear of mosquitoes. But Ireland didn't have those magical globes of childhood dreams called fireflies, either, so I supposed it was a fair trade. It wasn't even that hot outside, but hardly any of the buildings had air conditioning, so it was automatically a few degrees hotter in these ancient buildings.

Aidan was holding a tube of Pringles, which had apparently made the Atlantic jump, albeit in a flavor ominously called "prawn cocktail," and he was shaking it noisily.

"We need to start looking!" he demanded for the

fourth time that morning, wielding his Pringles can like a scepter. While most of us were more concerned with the sweat sticking our shirts to our backs, Aidan couldn't stop thinking about the visit with Colm yesterday. He'd spent all evening rehashing everything Colm had said, as if any of us had not been there. He even had a notebook in which he was keeping notes. It was the one I'd seen him with in the guest room at my house, and I wondered what he'd been writing that night.

Maybe: *Big house, nice beds, but the girl ain't talking.*

"We will start your futile search in a while," Rory said, exasperated. "Just give me a chance to rest. I have to work later."

"I just flew across an ocean to tell you you're a mythical creature, and you have to work?" Aidan asked.

"Who says mythical creatures don't have to pay rent?" Rory spat.

Rosie raised her eyes at me in amusement. We'd learned to stay out of it when Rory and Aidan started a sibling skirmish, otherwise I was sure Rosie would have made a mocking *rawr* sound.

"I don't trust that Colm Vesey. We need to check all the boat companies in Galway. We have to find—"

"Oh, my *god*, Aidan! Repeating it one more time is not going to get us *anywhere*."

Rosie and I sat in front of the windows, fanning ourselves with a pair of leaflets some dude with dreads was handing out on the street yesterday.

"Dear *god!*" Rosie shrieked. "Is Ireland always this hot in the summer?"

"Not at all." Rory sighed, falling into one of the black leather couches between Aidan and Rex. "I blame this weather on you guys. You brought it from the U.S." He looked over Aidan's shoulder as Aidan tapped away on Rory's laptop, scouring for boat companies that operated on the Corrib River, the river that wound through the heart of Galway.

*Harry Potter and the Order of the Phoenix* was playing on the TV. In Irish.

"… tá réim mothúchán spúnóg agat …" Hermione said.

"Damn it!" I yelped.

"What?" Rosie looked alarmed as she pointed to the TV. "You actually understood that?"

"What? No. I forgot to ask Colm what Aidan's real name is."

"It's Aidan," Rory said in a flat voice.

"What in the world are they saying?" Rosie asked as Hermione silently mouthed words at Ron and Harry, a voice dubbed over it speaking the strange, lyrical language.

"How do you not know *Harry Potter* by heart?" Rory said. "Hermione just told Ron he has the emotional range of a teaspoon."

"My, we are a bunch of nerds, aren't we?"

We all spun around to the strange voice—well, everyone but Rory, who said, "Hey, man," without turning around.

A boy with light brown hair gelled into an impressive swoop stood in the doorway, a green athletic bag slung over his shoulder. And then my stomach slid to my feet. A girl with long, wavy brown hair appeared behind him. She wore a long, thin skirt and one of those lacey tops that end in a position so as to reveal a good inch of your stomach. Hers, of course, was flat.

"Hello!" she called brightly, shoving into the room behind the guy that still stood in the doorway.

Rex hopped up at the commotion and ran gleefully toward the newcomers. The boy knelt and scooped up the tiny dog. "How's my wittlekins?"

"How's it going?" the girl said to the room at large, dropping her bags on the floor.

"I thought you lived with three boys," I muttered to what I thought was myself.

But Rory heard me and quirked his eyebrows. "I did. The three of us just moved into this apartment for the summer."

"Hi, I'm Rosie!" my boisterous friend proclaimed, oblivious to my nerves, flipping her luscious auburn hair over her shoulder.

"I'm *Neeve*," the girl said, which I later learned was ridiculously spelled "Niamh." She came over to shake each of our hands, except for Rory, who got a muss of the hair. "And that lout is *Nile*." Unlike the Egyptian river, that was spelled "Niall."

"Howya." The boy plopped down on the empty couch, Rex tucked under his arm. It was a bit strange to hear the thick Irish accent coming from such a young guy, very much like I'd imagine a leprechaun would sound. But I kept that tidbit to myself. "What are ye Yanks up to today?"

"Oh, you know," Rory said, "just looking for our birth father who may or may not be a murderer. Typical Tuesday, right?"

Neither of the newcomers looked especially surprised, so I

assumed Rory had already debriefed them on the situation. My heart gave a quick twang like the strings of the guitar at the thought of Rory texting the gorgeous Niamh.

*My, my, Cora, aren't we the jealous one?*

"That must be mad craic," Niall said, pronouncing the last word like *crack*.

"What's 'craic'?" Rosie asked.

"A life-ruining drug," Niall said with a serious face. "Take it from Niamh here. She squandered away her youthful years on it. That's why she looks like she's ninety. The craic was ninety!"

Rosie and I look uncomprehendingly at each other as Niamh swatted Niall on the arm, and Rex reacted with a growl. *Good, he doesn't like you either.*

"It means like fun or entertainment or conversation," Rory explained. "So when the craic is ninety, you're having a lot of fun."

"But generally speaking, it's okay to ignore anything Niall says," Niamh assured us. "So, what's your next step?" she asked, turning to Rory. "On finding your dad?" Yeah, she'd definitely been kept up to date. I tried not to fume. That was definitely not attractive.

"We got a lead that he might work for a boat company in Galway," Aidan piped up, probably to get the pretty girl's attention. "I'm making a list now."

"Let's talk about what we're all *really* wondering: are you guys going out tonight?" Rosie was obviously jonesing for her next beer, disappointed in the lack of interest the rest of her travel group was exhibiting in that particular pastime. You know, in the face of fairy tales coming to life and the prospect of magic being real, beer just didn't seem all that exciting.

"Not tonight, we've both got to work," Niamh answered.

"Speaking of," Rory said with a flick of the remote, turning the TV off. "I've got to work at five. So we better get going if you're going to drag me all over the city today, Aidan."

With a list of phone numbers in hand, we headed out into the glorious afternoon. Aidan had spent quite a lot of time Googling Kieran Brownes, but nothing noteworthy came up in the region or anywhere in Ireland. But boats? That's something Galway did have. And plenty of them.

There were clouds in the sky but none of them had dared to touch that midday sun yet. We spent the rest of the afternoon wandering down Shop Street and the various alleys, nooks, and crannies that surrounded it, Rosie and I ducking into shops while Rory and Aidan each attacked the list of boat operators. With little luck.

While Aidan popped into the tour information centers we passed, Rory called each number on the list, inquiring of each person who answered about a Seamus O'Leary. Apparently nobody answered favorably because Rory ended the call each time with growing annoyance.

By four o'clock, we'd ended up down at the bottom of Shop Street, where it opened up to a large wide-open area Rory called "the Spanish Arch." The bricks made swirling patterns on the ground here and an ancient-looking wall with an arched walkway in the middle crossed one end of the area. And right on our left, cutting through the heart of the city, was the infamous River Corrib, Seamus O'Leary's temptress.

It met the sea here in a strong current, tumbling over the rocks and sticks and debris on the riverbed in the low tide. Out beyond the river the ocean stretched to the horizon in a blue haze. On the other side of the river there was a stretch of rocky beach and sand where a collection of small boats in all shapes and colors and decrepitude sat, some turned over and some resting on their hulls.

Rory was obviously ready to ditch the effort as he sat on the river wall, dangling his feet over the edge. We sat beside him, the water a good four feet below my sandals.

"So what do we do now?" Rory asked.

"Well, let's do these last two numbers," Aidan said.

Rosie lay back in the sun, her bare legs dangling over the edge, and seemed to doze. My legs hot beneath my jeans, I watched a dog clamber down the steps that were tucked beneath a bridge, right into the river, chasing after a stick that his person threw.

"That's The Claddagh over there," Rory said, breaking into my thoughts, and I realized with a happy twist of my heart that he was talking to me. For the first time since our almost-kiss, he wasn't acting awkward and tense. A hand shading my eyes, I followed where he was pointing, across the river. There was a thin strip of land across from us, dripping with people, and another, smaller stream on the other side of it. On the other side of *that* there was a house-lined street, a colorful line broken only by a church and a *giant* grotto dedicated to somebody obviously very pious. "Have you heard of Claddagh rings?"

I fought the urge not to roll my eyes. Of course I had. The little ring consisting of two tiny hands clutching a heart between them, a crown set on top of it, had been the *in* thing to get at our high school as soon as you got a boyfriend, so, of course, I'd never gotten one. Though I'd always lusted after the things. I kept this to myself and just nodded.

"They come from here," Rory explained. "This area of town, specifically."

"That's so cool!" Rosie chirped from behind us, where she lay. "I have a couple of those! I don't even remember who gave them to me." She laughed as if this was so amusing, the fact that she'd had so many boyfriends in high school she couldn't even remember who'd given her a beautiful piece of jewelry.

And how many times had I lusted after Rosie's Claddagh rings, and my other classmates' rings, for that matter?

"It's really a thing in St. Louis?" Rory asked, surprised.

"Well, it was at our high school," Rosie said.

I pressed my lips into a tight line, trying desperately to pretend this conversation didn't bother me. That I couldn't still ardently feel the longing I'd held for so many years to get one of those rings from Josh Watson.

"Whenever you got a boyfriend, you were supposed to make him get you one. Otherwise he wasn't considered a boyfriend worth having," Rosie said with a chuckle. "Mine were really cheap, though. Cora, you never had one, did you?"

Two fires came alight, one on either side of my face, and I tried to contain the urge to push her right into the river. Maybe the dog would save her, if she was lucky.

Rory's gaze was heavy on my face, but he must have noticed my humiliation, because he said, "Our brother Declan is going to come out here." He turned to Aidan. "He texted, he wants to see you, bro."

Aidan had just finished a conversation with the final phone number on the list and threw his phone angrily in the grass behind him. "Nothing," he muttered.

"Uh, did you hear me?" Rory repeated. "Your loving, caring older brother—not me—is dying to see you."

"Yeah, yeah, wonderful," Aidan muttered. "That doesn't get us anywhere with Operation Selkie."

A muscle in Rory's jaw ticked, and I wondered if it had anything to do with the preference Aidan was showing for his newfound family over the one he'd grown up with. "Mr. and Mrs. O'Brien" he'd called them the other day.

"Operation Selkie? That is *so* not becoming a thing," Rosie said. "I'm not saying that word in public. How about Operation Who's Yer Daddy?"

"Maybe if we walk up and down the river?" Aidan suggested, his mind clearly one-track right now. "We might see something we missed."

"There's nothing on the river here," Rory told him. "The boats operate way up river, out of town."

"Well, I can try anyway." Aidan moved to get up, but suddenly fell to the ground with an *oof!*

"You are my sunshine! My only sunshine! You make me *happy*—"

A strange man was on top of Aidan, singing at the top of his lungs.

"Uh, should we be helping him?" Rosie asked, still lying down.

"Get off!" Aidan yelped, twisting around on the ground.

"When skies are gray!"

Rory chuckled, sweeping an arm out toward the rolling wrestlers. "Meet our brother Declan."

The guy jumped off Aidan, lowering into a dramatic bow. His dirty blond hair flopped over his eyes and he brushed it back with a flip of his head. "Wonderful to meet you, ladies." His accent was a strange mixture of American and Irish, like a constant battle was being waged between the two, certain words falling to one side or the other. "Our little Aido here used to walk around the house belting out that song."

Aidan wiped at a grass stain on his t-shirt. "I hope you do laundry better than you sing."

Rory laughed.

"And what exactly are you laughing about, dear brother?" Declan said, grabbing Rory around the middle and lugging him backward. "Ain't no mountain high enough! Ain't no valley low enough! Ain't no river wide enough!"

Laughter erupted from my stomach. There was nothing on this planet more adorable than the image of a baby Rory strutting around the resort singing like Diana Ross.

"Get off!

"What? No show for us today?"

"Cut it out, Dec, we don't have the time today," Aidan said, annoyed.

"Oh, no?" Declan said, forcing Rory to his feet to dance around to silent music. "Do my baby brothers have a double date tonight?" His eyebrows arced as he eyed me and Rosie.

"No!" Rosie chirped, her signature flirt-with-me smile pasted to her face. "He means finding his dad or whatever."

"Huh?"

"Finding Dad … uh …"

"A souvenir. A present," Rory said quickly. "Isn't his birthday coming up?"

"Yeah, I guess January is coming up eventually," Declan said, a suspicious look on his face. Things could have gone downhill from there with Rory and Aidan desperately trying to cover up their real business in Galway, but the universe deemed to save them. By throwing me under the bus.

"Yiiiiieeeeeeewww! Cora!" Rosie squawked.

My wonderful mood took a dangerous plummet as a strange feeling slid down my head to the tune of Rosie's almighty shriek.

All eyes swiveled to her, and we registered at once the way she was pointing at my hair, her nose scrunched and her eyes full of horror. I put a hand to my head and it came away white and wet.

*Oh god, no.*

Aidan snorted involuntarily and clapped a hand over his nose, but I had no time to send daggers his way, because a new sensation joined the wet one on my head. All of a sudden something was poking at my head. Something wet.

"Ew! He's eating the bird shit!" Rosie shrieked.

I turned and the dog from the river licked me full in the face. Reeling backward, I nearly toppled into the river, but Rory caught me by the arm just in time. He shooed the dog away from my head.

"Ewww!" Rosie's shrill voice was no doubt heard by everyone in the vicinity, and I would have strangled her if I wasn't going through such an embarrassing crisis.

"Chill, Rosie!" snapped Rory, my knight in shining, un-pooped-upon armor. After helping me stand, he released my arm, and the joy of his touch disappeared with the growing realization that a bird had just released its bowels upon my head. In public. In front of Rory.

*He'll never kiss me now.* I took a deep breath. *It could have happened to anybody,* I told myself carefully, willing the tears to stay out of my eyes.

"Are you okay?" Rory asked, as if bird poop could have a velocity so as to injure my skull.

"Uh-huh," I half groaned, half croaked.

"As much fun as this is," Declan said, waving an arm in my general direction. "What are your plans for the evening?

"I have to get to work," Rory said. He studied my face, probably trying to ascertain whether or not I was going to hold it together, and held his keys out to Aidan. "And Cora needs to shower."

"Here, I brought the spare you gave me," Declan said, handing Aidan a trio of keys on a plastic flag keychain checkered maroon and white.

"Cool." Rory pocketed his keys. "Are you okay?" he asked me again.

I couldn't manage anything more than a nod.

"Okay. Then I'll see you guys later." He gave me one last look full of pity before heading off across the patio toward Shop Street.

"Well!" Declan said, clapping his hands together. "Mum called me yesterday to inform me of your little stunt, Aido, and begged me to talk some sense into you. Naturally, I'm here to do so. Pub? Who's coming?"

What a responsible big brother. Not to mention I was still wearing shit. A lot of it.

"I'm up for it," Aidan said. He scrunched up the failed phone numbers and tossed them into one of those big, black trash cans that said *bruscar*, which Aidan had told us was Irish for something trash-related.

"I'd love to!" Rosie chirped.

*Traitor*, I thought darkly. I still wanted to strangle her but that yearning came second to the burning need to remove the poop from my head.

"Uh, I think I need to go back to the apartment," I said, pointing a finger at my head.

"Oh, right." Rosie's eyebrows scrunched together. "Would you be, uh … would you mind if …"

"No, go ahead. I'm tired, anyway. I'll see you guys later." Aidan handed me the spare keys as Declan held his hooked arms out on either side of him. Rosie and Aidan each threaded an arm through one of his and the trio skipped off down the freaking yellow-brown brick road.

# *Geit Mór*
# A MIGHTY SHOCK

I SAT IN RORY'S ROOM AFTER SHOWERING THE SHIT out of my hair. Now that his roommates were back, Rosie and I would stay in his room while he and Aidan took the couches.

Our bags sat at the end of the bed, mine spilling bland t-shirts next to Rosie's array of colorful silks and dresses. I picked out a t-shirt from our senior year of high school and pulled it on with some athletic shorts, my sleepwear of choice. As I dug to find a pair of socks, I came across the envelope from dad's office with the bus times scribbled across it.

My dad's strange behavior on the phone filled my mind. Rosie agreed. Our fathers weren't the type to care about money. I pulled on a pair of pink socks that each sported the face of a bunny on the toes before ripping open the envelope.

Sliding out the neatly folded letter inside, I noticed the stationery was very fancy. And from a law firm.

My brain, still addled from embarrassment, stumbled over the long legal words and Latin phrases. A few key phrases punched my eyes as if they were highlighted. With pitchforks.

*Notice to appear*

*brings this suit against Francis Manchester of Fullington Factory, Inc.*

*breach of contract*

I gulped. *Suit? Breach of contract?* Somebody was suing my dad.

It was like I'd just been shit on all over again.

"Whoa! Sorry! I didn't know you were here!"

Snapping my head up, I shoved my bunny socks under my butt as Rory took a few steps backward. "Oh, I can get out of here if you need the room," I said quickly.

"No, no, I was just going to grab some clothes for a shower." He paused and took in the letter in my hands and probably the distressed look on my face. "Aidan texted that you all went out with Declan, I didn't expect anybody to be home."

"I, uh, had the issue to take care of." I gestured toward my wet hair that lay limp and tangled on my shoulder.

"Oh, right." He nodded.

*Wonderful.* He'd forgotten about my shitty head and I'd just brought it up again.

"We were overstaffed tonight. Slow night. They let me off."

I nodded, pressing my lips into a straight line and willing myself to listen to his words instead of dwelling on the officious letter in my hands. But a cold fist still clenched my heart, making it difficult to breathe.

Rory stepped over to the bed and perched softly on the edge. "Are you okay?"

I leaned back against the pillows, each one bearing a logo I didn't recognize. It didn't take me long to decide to tell him. The sheer number of times he'd seen me crying last summer made him automatically qualified to deal with an upset Cora. "Somebody's suing my dad," I said, handing him the letter.

His eyebrows lifted as he scanned the document. "Whoa."

"Yeah. Whoa," I murmured.

"Did ... does he know that you know?"

It was mighty suspicious the way I had this letter with me, halfway across the world. I shook my head.

"You gotta tell him."

I nodded. "I know."

Rory pitched the letter on the bed as if it was poisonous and moved to sit next to me. But when he reached for a pillow to move it against the headboard, he cussed and whipped his hand back like he'd been burned.

"What happened?" I asked.

"Something shocked me," he said. We looked at each other for a long moment and then he slowly reached out and lifted the pillow up by the pillowcase.

Laying innocently beneath it was the sealskin.

"Aidan!" Rory groaned.

I wanted to snicker at Aidan's ingenuity but something sinister remained. "It hurt you?" I asked, incredulous.

He nodded. We looked at each other, then at the sealskin, and then back at each other. He nodded slightly and then reached his hand toward the skin.

"Be careful," I said, inching backward toward the edge of the bed.

When the tips of his fingers made contact with the skin, there was the slightest sizzling sound which disappeared in a nanosecond. He yanked his hand back once again.

"Ow!" He shook his hand as if that would dispel the pain. "Why did that little jerk stash it under my pillow if it was going to burn me? What's happening?"

"I don't know," I breathed. "But I do know that didn't happen when Aidan touched it."

Fear welled in his eyes and I wanted more than anything to be able to calm it. To massage away the wrinkle between his eyebrows.

"Cora, I'm a little scared."

The cold fist clenched harder on my heart. He wasn't supposed to say that! *I* was the one that was jumpy and cried all the time. That's the way this worked!

"That's not good," I said softly. "'Cause I'm scared, too."

We both stared at the skin, willing it to act again, to give some hint of its secrets. But nothing happened.

"Let's look at this reasonably," I said, taking a deep breath. "Logic. Logic can solve anything."

He gave me an *oh please* look. "Logic left us a long time ago."

My eyebrows skyrocketed. "Excuse me? I thought you didn't believe in all this," I said.

"Well, my hand believes something right now!" he cried, clutching his twice-shocked hand in the other.

"Okay, logic," I repeated. "Just because weird shit is happening, doesn't mean we can't use logic."

"Be my guest," he said darkly.

"Well, if Aidan's skin is here, in Ireland ... Then that—that's yours." Which didn't exactly explain why it was attempting to burn him alive. "So that must mean that—that shock thing is *supposed* to happen."

"This is insane," he muttered, nearly inaudible.

"No kidding."

His hand trembled as he moved it, in a claw, toward the skin again. This time, when the sizzling sound erupted, he didn't move his hand away. I glanced at his grimace before looking back at the skin, breathlessly waiting for what would happen next.

And it didn't disappoint.

The edges of the skin seemed to be blending into his hand.

"Oh god! Oh god!" Rory jumped up—and the skin went with him. He whipped his hand around as if to put out flames, the skin flying behind him like a morbid Superman cape.

I jumped to my feet, fear gripping my throat and the blankets twisted around my feet. "Rory, calm down, it's okay!" I yelped to no avail. My tone disagreed with my words. After all, I had no idea if it was okay!

"Bullshit!" he nearly screamed, dancing around the room in a ghastly two-step. I dashed about the bed, a good two feet taller than him from this vantage point. I reached to grab his hands, to calm him, but I was a little scared to reach him.

Rory froze all of a sudden, in the middle of this terrible dance. Without thinking, he grabbed the sealskin with his free hand and wrenched it away from himself, his knuckles white with the force. But the thing stuck to his other hand.

I leaped from the bed and grabbed it, tugging hard, and when it finally ripped free of his hand, the sealskin flew across the room. Mouth hanging open, I took a few steps backward and sat on the bed.

He stood, panting, staring down at his hand, which was left with a big red welt where contact had been made—and forcibly removed. Chest heaving, his eyes rose to meet mine. I clamped my mouth shut, hoping to restore some calm to the room, but my breath was coming too fast, as well.

Rory sat down on the bed against the headboard and heaved his legs on top of the blanket. He cradled his angry red hand with his other. I crawled up beside him and hesitated only a moment before snaking an arm around his shoulders. He immediately collapsed into me, his head laying heavy on my shoulder.

"It's okay," I said breathlessly, pushing a splash of brown hair away from his forehead. Despite the circumstances of the embrace, my heart stumbled around like a drunk elephant.

"I didn't want to believe," he whispered, not opening his eyes.

"I know," I said. "It's some messed up shit."

He snorted. "You can say that again."

"It's some messed up shit," I said, trying to lighten the mood. The sealskin lay in a heap near the bank of windows, pooled in a macabre heap on the floor in front of the cheery white curtains. There was no way I would touch that thing. Even though the way it hadn't affected Aidan was a pretty good clue that nothing would happen if I *did* touch it, there was no way I was going to.

After a few minutes Rory sat up, his face a carefully constructed mask of indifference. He gestured toward the navy blue night outside the windows. "They use that street like a highway," he said.

The sky outside was lit from below by the streetlights that lined Shop Street, and flashing past the window in abrupt glimmers of white was seagull after seagull. A seagull highway.

Rory obviously wanted to change the subject, but I wasn't quite ready to relinquish it yet.

"Do you believe now?" I asked softly. "Ronan?"

The mask on Rory's face fell to pain and confusion. He wasn't angry, but he whispered, "Please don't call me that."

I gulped and laid my head on his shoulder before we could regress any farther. "Okay." He leaned his cheek against the top of my head, and I fell asleep to the rapid beating of his heart.

# *An Scrúdú*
# THE TEST

T HE WONDERFULLY FAMILIAR SMELL OF HIM WAS everywhere, but when I opened my eyes, Rosie was lying in his place. While I was cocooned inside the comforter, Rosie was sprawled next to me on top of the covers.

*Rory.* Where was he? Was he okay? Was his hand still red and hurt, evidence of the freaky events of last night? I made an attempt to get out of bed quietly, but Rosie woke up when I stirred.

"Wha'time is it?" she grumbled, propping herself up on her elbows.

"No clue," I said, checking my phone for the time and trying to check my disappointment at not finding Rory beside me.

I got up to change into jeans and maybe something

that wasn't a t-shirt, when the full attack of emotions from last night came rushing at my head. That crazy sealskin stuff wasn't my only problem.

"Shit," I muttered. After I found Rory, I needed to call my dad. What if he didn't even know about the lawsuit? After all, I'd taken the letter from his desk, unopened.

"Hey, Cora?"

"Hmm?" I zipped up my jeans and turned around to find Rosie sitting upright in the bed, studying her nails, her eyebrows drawn low over her bloodshot eyes. Her nails were always perfectly manicured, so there was no reason to inspect them. Something was wrong.

"Could you do me a favor?"

"Um, sure. What is it?" I sat down on the bed beside her.

Her face was full of … well, shame. She opened her mouth to speak then just expelled a bunch of air instead.

"God, you didn't hook up with Declan did you?" Not exactly a thoughtful thing to say when your best friend is clearly struggling with something, but if that something was remorse for hooking up with one of Rory's brothers, I was going to strangle her. "Rosie?"

She shook her head. "No. I just need you to pick me up something from the store."

"Whew, I can do that. I'll go get us some breakfast while I'm out." *And find Rory.* "What do you need?" *Tampons? Toothpaste? Shampoo?* I could cover any of those bases. But the pink of the blush left on her cheeks from last night was deepening to an ominous scarlet.

"I need a pregnancy test."

One catastrophe at a time. I moved nervously up Shop Street toward Eyre Square. I'd never bought a pregnancy test in the United States, much less a foreign country, but I figured my best bet was a chemist. Because I hadn't run into Aidan or Rory in the apartment, I refused to go to any of the busy chemists on Shop Street, especially not the one below Rory's apartment, in case they were around. I wanted my mortification to be contained to as few people as possible.

What I was looking for was tucked between two rows of houses a solid eight minutes' walk from Shop Street. The short, white-painted walls on either side of it created a tiny patio in front of the little pharmacy. I paused there to gather my courage and pretend to study the big sign above the door that proclaimed "Conneely's Chemist" in fake mosaics.

*Just don't ramble*, I thought, though telling myself that was a bit like telling a cow not to moo.

A little bell dinged over the door, as my eyes took in the miniscule room. The walls lined with full shelves and tiny fine print made it seem even smaller, and the counter dwarfed the space. And behind it stood none other than Santa Claus.

My cheeks turned to tomatoes as he greeted me much as I assumed Santa himself would have.

"Welcome, welcome! What can I do you fer?" he asked, rubbing one of his ruddy cheeks. Behind him there was a wide doorway that led into a bright, airy room where another pharmacist worked away.

"I—uh … um …" A hand flew to my temple as if to feign thinking. *Lie. You can lie right now. Make Rosie come back for it herself.* But the amount of fear I'd seen in Rosie's eyes pushed the thought out of me. Rosie. The brave one. The courageous one. She was leaning on me for once.

"I need a pregnancy test," I said softly.

The jolly old man let out a chuckle which caused his white beard to bounce like falling snow. "No need to look so down, my dear. Come to the back, we'll get you set up."

*So much for conservative Irish stereotypes*, I thought, as I followed him through the doorway behind the counter. Two pharmacists lifted a hand in greeting before turning back to their work. He stopped at part of the high, pristine counter that lined this room. It came up to his chest.

"Yer American, aren't you?" Santa said lightly, as he brought several boxes down from a shelf high above us.

*Yep, that's me. Spreading that stupid American-girls-are-easy rumor around the world.* I merely nodded. Keeping my mouth shut was the best way to avoid rambling.

"I've got cousins in Boston," he said with a smile. *Doesn't everybody in Ireland?* "I was there once. Years and years ago. I was in New York, too. Biggest city I've ever seen. Which do you want?" He changed topics so quickly I was caught off guard.

"Uh, I … It doesn't matter. It's not for me," I added quickly.

"Of course, of course," he said knowingly.

"No, really, it's for a friend." *Jesus, find some more clichés.*

"Well, tell your friend that it has a ninety-nine percent accuracy rate. And that it's most accurate about two weeks after"—*please don't say it*—"ovulation."

I nodded mutely.

"And you—I mean, your *friend*, should wait—"

"It is for my friend!" I interrupted frantically. "I swear!"

"Okay, okay. Just make sure your friend"—here he winked—"waits to use the test until menstruation should have started."

The last thing I wanted to hear coming out of Santa's mouth was the word *menstruation* one more time. I had to get out of there!

"Awesome, thanks a million. How much do I owe you?"

After a five-minute elaboration on his trip to New York, I was able to slip away. But it was the most embarrassing ten minutes of my life. Rosie was going to pay. Big time. That is, if she wasn't already paying in other, far more serious ways.

I handed Rosie the paper bag. She just stared at it.

"Well?"

"Thanks, Cora." She stared at the bag in her hands as though it was the remains of a beloved pet.

"Um, I'm kind of dying to know, so, could you … uh …?"

Rosie nodded mutely and left the room without looking at me. The action made my heart hurt. Those blue eyes of Rosie's were known for their roving, moving about the room and boring into your soul, bringing forth your most inner thoughts. Those eyes could set you to dancing just by looking at you. But today, they were the saddest I'd ever seen them. I plopped down on the bed to wait, my heart racing as though it was the contents of *my* uterus being questioned.

She returned just a few moments later and sat down on the bed next to me, holding the little white stick out like it was toxic.

We stared at it.

I didn't bother asking how long we had to wait—I figured we'd know when it was time.

And then a single line appeared, intersecting the little oval window completely.

"What does that mean?"

"I don't know," Rosie breathed, bringing it closer to her face as though that would clear everything up.

"Is that a minus sign or, like, the 'yes' box?" I demanded, my voice rising.

"I don't know!" Rosie shrieked.

"Didn't you read the directions?" I yelped, scrambling around the bed for the empty box.

"Of course I did! But I was nervous! I don't remember!"

"Where is it?"

Rosie blanched. "I left it in the bathroom."

We both darted for the door at the same time, painfully squeezing through the doorway. As we launched into the hall as one, we came into contact with a thin figure.

"Jaysus! Where's the fire?" Niall demanded, just barely keeping his feet.

"Sorry," I mumbled, as Rosie dashed ahead. I followed her at what I hoped seemed a normal pace. But when I turned the corner to the bathroom, I bumped straight into Rosie's back.

Rory stood in the door of the bathroom, the empty pregnancy test box in his hand.

*Oh dear Santa of pregnancy tests, all I want for Christmas is my dignity back!*

"That's not—" What? Mine? No shit, Cora.

"I sort of need that," Rosie whispered, carefully taking the box from Rory's grasp and scurrying back to the bedroom.

My nerves could only take a moment longer of looking at his embarrassed, shocked face before racing back to his room. I shut the door and leaned against it, all energy leaking out of me. Just how many times was I going to have to endure humiliation in front of Rory?

"The appearance of two lines indicate a pregnancy," Rosie read aloud. "One line indicates the absence of a pregnancy."

At the same time that relief flooded me, a trio of tears escaped Rosie's blue eyes.

Sighing, I sat down next to her, pulling her against me with an arm around her shoulders. I knew tears weren't the release of sadness—they were the exhausted result of suppressing it too long—but still her distress made me nervous. "That's good, Roz."

She sniffled and wiped the tears from her eyes. They left a blurry charcoal trail across her cheeks from last night's makeup. "But," she whispered, "sometimes they're wrong."

"And sometimes they're right." *Great logic, Cora.* With all the drama in my life lately, I seriously needed to invest in some comforting-your-friends classes. "We can get another one in a few days," I said.

She nodded against my shoulder.

"Was it … Luke?" I asked.

"Jesus, Cora! Of course it was Luke! I'm not sleeping with the *entire* frat!" She sat up and inched away from me, anger creasing her forehead.

"No, I didn't mean …" But there was no point arguing. She knew that compared to mine, her sex life was exotic. Besides, I preferred to see the anger written across her face rather than the debilitating fear of before. "Why on earth did you wait until we were halfway across the world to tell me you thought you might be pregnant? Why couldn't we have done this in the comfort of our own home? Our own Walgreens?"

"And have our parents sniffing around?"

"And Rosie, if you knew you might be pregnant, why did you go out drinking last night? That was really, really not—"

"What? Responsible? And possibly getting pregnant was? Besides, when have I ever been responsible?"

"Well, soon you might have to be." The words were out before I could stop them. She looked like I'd slapped her. Which I might as well have. "But, uh, probably not," I added lamely.

She sniffed and wiped at her face, which only spread the mascara tracks around her cheeks.

"Are you going to tell Luke?" I asked as gently as possible.

She shook her head, her shoulders slumping a fraction of an inch. "Unless the test turns out to be wrong."

# *Fós*
## STILL

RORY WAS IN THE SITTING ROOM WITH HIS GUITAR when Rosie and I finally emerged. His eyes flitted to Rosie, but he didn't say anything.

"Where's Aidan?" I asked, trying to set the bar for a normal conversation. You know, as normal as we could get these days. I'd have to call my dad later, and maybe talk to Rory about last night. But for now, normal would be great.

"He's out walking up and down the river," Rory said. He didn't even seem to notice he was strumming gently on the guitar; he did so almost unconsciously. "He insists on working this little mystery every minute he gets. Even though there's nothing to find on that river."

"He's really … *committed* to this," I said, trying to avoid the words "crazy" and "insane."

"He's making himself sick," Rory said. "He's not going to find Seamus. And what's he going to do once he has the other skin? It's probably going to—" I knew he was about to reference the events of last night, but his eyes found Rosie once more and he shut his mouth. He cleared his throat and asked, "Did you call your dad?"

I shook my head. "Sort of nervous," I said. The fact that Rosie didn't even ask what we were talking about was proof of her altered state of mind.

"How's your hand?" I ventured.

"Fine," he said, and his voice was vaguely angry. His fingers danced across the strings of his guitar, giving us a soft, quick melody as he stared absently out the window. I could see the red on his hand, just a blur as he played.

"That's really pretty," I said, trying to get us back on that plane we'd been on last night where we could talk and hold each other and be like we used to be.

But for some reason, those simple words made him stop abruptly. His fingers jerked away from the strings with a soft, discordant sound and he roughly set the guitar on the couch next to him.

"When did you learn to play guitar?" I asked.

"My brother Declan started teaching me back when I was staying with him. I thought I mentioned that in one of my emails …"

*Ouch.* He most definitely hadn't mentioned that, because I could recite those emails like the Pledge of Allegiance. But his point was clear: maybe, if I hadn't broken off that email chain, our one lifeline, he would have told me. Maybe he'd have played for me over Skype.

Maybe maybe maybe. I was beginning to understand there were a lot of those in life.

Obviously realizing his comments had rendered me silent, he stood up. "Lunch?"

"Please!" Rosie yelped. "Somebody in this body is hungry."

"Nothing," Aidan muttered as he collapsed into the chair next to Rosie's. His crooked front tooth made him look even younger than he was and petulant. "Absolutely nothing." We'd already ordered our lunches by the time Aidan appeared, looking more defeated than the losing team in game seven of the World Series.

"Told you," Rory said, taking a sip of his Coke. "Aido, he could be dead for all we know."

As if to fuel the fire between the siblings, Griffin's Bakery had seen fit, despite the season, to light the old fireplaces that adorned its many rooms. "It's June!" Rosie had cried in exasperation when we first sat down. It was almost like Ireland didn't know how to handle the warmth. We were on the second floor at a table facing a fireplace, a big window overlooking Shop Street to my right. It was overcast today, but warmth still lingered under those clouds.

Aidan opened a menu only to slam it shut again moments later. "I'm not hungry," he mumbled.

"Really? Don't seals need to eat like a pound of fish every day?" Rosie said sardonically.

Aidan only glared at her.

Luckily our trio of sandwiches was served soon, probably in an attempt to turn over the table to another group of tourists during the heavy lunch rush. The meal was tense, thanks in no small part to Rosie's biting sarcasm interspersed with unnatural quiet.

"These are, like, sour cream and onion or something," I said, holding up a potato chip from my plate. "What a weird default to serve with a sandwich."

Rory raised his eyebrows, a smirk playing around the corner of his lips.

I looked to Rosie for backup but she was staring at the crusts of her chicken sandwich like they were made of anchovies.

"Yeah, I mean, it's bizarre not to just serve the normal, salted flavor," I went on in my tireless crusade to make my freaked-out friends talk about something as mundane as lunch. "What if I don't like sour cream and onion chips?

"Crisps," Rory corrected.

I laughed but it was drowned out by the sound of Aidan's chair scraping backward. He stood quickly, an annoyed look on his face. "I'm gonna go look some more," he muttered before stalking off.

"Should we—"

Lord only knows how I intended to finish that sentence, because Rosie jumped to her feet then, too. "I'm going to help him," she said before tossing her crumpled napkin on the table and hurrying after him.

Well, my friends were having a wonderful summer. Was Rory

going to freak out next? I glanced at the red mark still on his hand, then up at the little gap between his lips, where my eyes lingered.

"Why is he freaking out so much?" he said. The movement of his lips snapped me out of my embarrassing trance.

*Maybe because your birth father is possibly still alive, contrary to popular belief, your mother is a woman you've known your whole life as a neighbor, and a story from Irish folklore that challenges everything we've ever known appears to be true?* But saying that out loud wasn't going to get us anywhere.

Instead, I just shrugged. "I guess it means a lot to him," I murmured.

"It means a lot to me, too," Rory said, "but Jesus. He's making himself sick."

But I couldn't help thinking it seemed as though all this *didn't* mean a lot to Rory. He never acted as though it did. He still went to work just like every other day and spent hours and hours appearing to not be thinking about it at all.

"Let's go find that psycho brother of mine," he said. "And your equally unhinged friend."

At a tiny cash register in the corner, he paid for the entire uneaten meal, including the dine-and-dasher's, and pushed away my money when I tried to offer a handful of coins. Who knows how much was in there, I would never get the hang of two-euro coins.

"Thanks," I mumbled, following him down the rickety stairs and out into the cloudy day. He headed down Shop Street toward the river, but just before we reached the end, he tugged on my hand, which lit up at the contact.

"Come here," he said, ducking into a stone-paved alley between a bar and a restaurant. A sign on the side of the restaurant proclaimed "Druid Lane."

"Druids, huh?" I said. "If selkies exist, maybe druids do, too."

He didn't answer, or even look at me.

The buildings weren't tall, but there was no sunlight to be blocked out anyway. The alley was shrouded in darkness. Just as it began to curve to the right, the stone wall gave way to a glass wall.

"What the—?"

Rory chuckled at my surprise. There was an open glass door, and he stepped through onto a raised metal walkway. "It's a dig site," he said, nodding for me to follow. A roof with floodlights affixed enclosed the entire space, which opened up to a parking lot on the other side. Giant circles of light illuminated patches of artifacts as we walked through.

There was a great open pit beside the walkway, and on the other side of that was an office with a glass wall. People worked on computers there, completely ignoring us, under a sign that declared "Halla an Iarla Rua."

"The Hall of the Red Earl," Rory said. "It's this thirteenth-century hall where people used to come to seek help from the family that ruled the city, or to prove their fealty."

"That's very *Game of Thrones*," I said.

Rory laughed. "Yeah, but instead of the Starks they were looking for help from the de Burgos. Not sure they had anything as exciting as direwolves." His footsteps clinked on the metal. "It would've helped, though. They were from England and some Celtic tribes finally took the city."

The walkway twisted down some stairs into the pit where a series of ancient-looking stones formed giant rectangles, the foundation of the former hall.

"They didn't even know it was here until the '90's when they were trying to build something here. So they left it and built on stilts above instead." Rory pointed upward at the ceiling that apparently held a building overhead.

"Ireland's just full of surprises," I breathed.

Rory's amused chuckled made my heart sing. "You have no idea," he said.

"I guess I was a bit of a surprise, too, huh?" I said quietly.

The sound of his laughter had built my courage up enough to say something I'd been thinking for a while, but when he went silent, I immediately regretted it.

"A little bit," he finally said.

We were standing at the end of the metal walkway at the side of the pit, near a huge cruciform stone that was added to the ruinous hall for ironworking after the de Burgo family lost power, according to a plaque I read to avoid looking Rory in the eyes.

"I'm sorry," I said. "For not telling you I was coming. I just … I really wanted to see you again."

The tip of a white tooth appeared on his lip, nibbling in … what? Nervousness? Awkwardness?

It didn't matter because the emotions that must have played out in this hall, emanating from this ruin now, were seeping into my skin, and speedboat-mouth Cora was alive and well. "And I'm … I'm sorry I didn't tell you about the selkie thing, I was scared. I didn't know how to tell you. And I should've told you I was coming, but Aidan convinced me … and …"

*Stop the excuses, Cora.* Because that's what those were. Just excuses. *Tell the truth.*

"And I missed you."

There it was. The meat of the matter, sitting out in the ruins of a once-glorious hall where fine feasts were had. Just like a starving peasant in the 1200's, I was prepared to beg.

"I still think about you all the time, Rory. God, I missed you so much. I know I never said it last year, but I … I think I love you."

His brown eyes glistened in the floodlights, and for just a moment he did seem like a ruler, wielding a power he didn't want to hold.

"Let's go find Aidan and Rosie," he said, leading the way back to Druid Lane.

It was going to take more than a druid to help me now.

# *An Rollchóstóir*
## THE ROLLER COASTER

WHEN RORY FINALLY LEFT FOR WORK, LOOKING darling in a black polo that read "The Quays" in white on the back, he left us all in the apartment, tense and quiet—Aidan most of all. Rosie disappeared and then Aidan left, and I found myself alone in the sitting room in a thankful, blissful solitude.

*Friends* was on TV, apparently a staple of Irish television, but I wasn't paying attention. My mind was too muddled to comprehend even a sitcom. I was no stranger to rejection, but how much more could I take? Getting turned down by every private college in the Midwest last year had been hard, but getting no response to the first time you said "I love you"? That was especially brutal. More painful than the time I sprained my wrist on the monkey bars. It didn't help that one day Rory was friendly and sweet and dare I say it, even *loving*—almost kissing me in the bathroom and snuggling up to me in his bed. But the next he was cold and apparently confused by my feelings and leaving me to listen to my own "I love you" echo around an ancient stone hall. This emotional roller coaster was getting to be too much. Just then, Rex jumped up onto the couch and laid his tiny head on my lap.

I scoffed. "Oh, so you like me now?" I demanded. "Just like that?" My fingers scratched the little dog's soft head, and the comforting doggy feeling made me homesick for Princess. "I guess I'll take it. Not many people are too happy to be around me right now."

Desperate for a distraction, I turned on the Wifi capability on my phone and was met with a satisfying barrage of *ding* notifications.

One was an email from my mom. With foreboding in my gut, I opened it. Surely she was out to chastise me, too. Even though I wasn't quite sure what a lecture from Mom about money would sound like.

But I was *so* wrong.

*Oh, Cora,* it read, *I do hope you're having a blast! Try and have fun with Rosie, I know she'll show you a good time. I assume you're there to see that boy, and I know I wasn't so supportive last summer, and after all that crying I liked him even less, but I trust you. Just make sure he's good for you, sweetie. And I would love you to bring me back some Belleek china if you find any. Maybe a nice plate or teapot or something to give Joan for her birthday. I just never know what to give that woman.*

"How about a raise?" I muttered.

*Anyway,* the note ended, *do try to have a good time, Cora! I love you and see you soon! Remember: Belleek!*

My nervous breath came out in a sigh, but for some reason that didn't dislodge the uncomfortable twist in my stomach. Sure, it was a relief, and kind of cool, that Mom was trusting me to choose my own boy, that was definitely a step forward from last summer. But if Dad was stressed out about money, why wasn't Mom yelling at me, too? Not a mention of anything but my life. Did she even know about the lawsuit? Or Dad's freak-out over money?

My parents' relationship had never seemed particularly serious or strong to me, but then again, I'd never had occasion to consider it before. Now I was. And I was worried.

The pad of my thumb was hovering over my dad's cell phone number when I heard a gut-wrenching sound. Literally.

Creeping toward the bathroom, I strained my ears to listen. And my suspicions were confirmed. Somebody was puking.

My chest felt suddenly cold and hollow. *Rosie.*

As I crept to the door, the apartment went silent. There were two obvious options here: go barge in and hold her hair back, or pretend I hadn't heard. More than anything I wanted to do my duty as a good friend, but as a good friend, I knew Rosie. She wouldn't want me in there. Fiercely independent, she would only ask me to leave. And that would hurt. I turned back toward the sitting room.

The retching sound came back with renewed vigor, followed by coughing. It pierced a hole in my heart.

I couldn't believe it. Rosie was right. *The test was wrong.*

With my phone in my hand, I went back to the quiet sitting room and sat nervously on the couch, my toes tapping an anxious medley on the floor. I could only deal with one crisis at a time, because I was beginning to unravel. Better to focus my powers to solve one at a time. Dialing the familiar number with the unfamiliar country code at the start, I waited.

And waited.

The answering machine finally picked up. My heartbeat leapt into overdrive. I knew what I'd say to my dad, but reciting it to a machine made me even more nervous for some reason.

*Beeeeep.*

"Hey, uh, hey, Dad. It's Cora. Obviously. Um, so I just wanted to tell you I found this, uh, this letter in my bag. Well I found it on your desk, but I accidentally put it in my bag." *Oh god. I sound like a klepto!* "I, anyway, I opened it to make sure it wasn't anything important that you needed. And, uh, I think it is." I gulped, but there was still an insurmountable lump in my throat so I gulped again. Then I got scared the answering machine was going to cut me off. "The letter says something about a lawsuit. So, if you could call me back, I'd—"

*Beeeeep.*

The words died on my trembling lips. Honesty was hard.

Putting my hands flat on the cool leather of the couch, I waited until my heartbeat slowed down. Sometime before it was totally back to normal, the door to the sitting room flew open.

Rosie plopped down beside me, rubbing her eyes and smearing clouds of eyeliner around her eyes. "How are you?" I said stupidly.

"Fine. Just woke up," she said with a convincing yawn.

She didn't want me to know. "Oh?" I said, playing along. "Where is everybody?"

Rosie shrugged. "Aidan said something about working the oceanfront."

"The ocean's a big place," I said. "He's really taking this badly, isn't he?"

We lapsed into silence as we watched American TV. It almost felt like we were at home, just hanging out. Before last year and the Summer that Changed Everything. But any movement, any lapse in focus on the TV and my consciousness came back in full swing to remind me that we were *not* two innocent seventeen-year-old girls. Nope. Nineteen-year-old Cora was quite different from the girl that had lusted after a Claddagh ring.

We saw two full *Friends* episodes before Rosie, apparently similarly uninterested in Rachel's antics, cried, "Cora, what the hell am I gonna declare for a major next year?" She looked absolutely stricken.

"Um ... I don't know?" The level of emotion in her voice and face wasn't commensurate with the topic at hand. I knew I had to tread carefully because it appeared we were working on some serious dual levels.

"I mean, I'm not good at *anything*! I don't even *like* anything! How am I supposed to choose something?"

"Rosie, that's not true—"

"Oh, really?" she demanded, her perfect eyebrows arched. "Do tell. What am I good at?"

"Oh, great, not putting me on the spot or anything."

Rosie snorted and folded her arms when I failed to come up with anything. "Like you're any better. What are you going to declare? Math? We both know what your ACT scores were."

"Hey!" I yelped angrily. "That was a low blow! What did I ever do to you?"

Why was she so worried about the future all of a sudden, anyway? She wasn't exactly the five-year-plan type of girl. "Live a little," she'd told me. She wasn't doing very well at that herself now.

"Maybe you could do business," she muttered. "Oh wait. You cried when our lemonade stand went bust."

"Okay, one"—I held up one angry finger—"it did not 'go bust.' You gave all the lemonade away to the sixth grade boys' soccer team. The entirety of whom, *by the way*, was entirely too old for you! And second, why is it Beat up on Cora Day?"

Twin *whooshes* of air left Rosie's delicate nostrils. "I just … what am I going to do?"

*Oh.* We were definitely not talking about majors.

"You don't have to do anything yet," I said softly. "Just, learn to live a little, Balducci."

She smirked but it was full of pain and didn't even show those pearly whites she loved to bare.

"Well," I tried again, "if it makes you feel any better, I messed up, too."

"You're pregnant?"

"Rosie, I'm pretty sure you have to have sex to get pregnant."

"Maybe your major could be health."

I stuck my tongue out at her.

"But seriously," she added, "how did you mess up?"

I sighed a deep, dramatic sigh. "I told Rory I loved him today."

"Shut up!"

"If only I could, that would have saved me from this mess in the first place." I sighed once more and rested my head back against the couch.

"Well? What did he say?"

"Let's just say *I* won't be in danger of getting pregnant any time soon." I smiled toothlessly, hoping to cheer her up.

Suddenly, the front door shut and Rory appeared in the doorway, his hair pushed aside and gleaming with sweat. He looked at each of our stunned faces. "Am I interrupting something?"

"No!" we both yelled at the same time.

He was startled, and I hoped he'd attribute our weird behavior to Rosie's recent … erm, *test*, and not the fact that I'd recently tried to hand him my heart and he'd politely pushed it away.

However, there is a God, because before anybody could utter one more damning syllable, the front door shut again. Only this time, it slammed, shaking the whole apartment and setting the old windows to tinkling gently in their frames.

"Guys! You guys! Cora! Rosie!"

Rosie and I were both on our feet by the time Aidan came bursting into the sitting room, nearly colliding with Rory.

"Rory!" he screeched, his breathing ragged. He doubled over to place his hands on his knees but he didn't stop to catch his breath. "I did it! I found him! I found Seamus O'Leary!"

# *Tuairim ar Deireadh*
## A LEAD AT LAST

WE ALL STARED AT HIM, STUNNED.

Aidan spun around the room, brandishing a colorful brochure at us. "He's not in Galway!" he yelled joyously. "That's why we couldn't find him! He's not in Galway City!"

Rosie took the brochure from him and her eyes flew over the front. Rory grabbed it from her and Aidan punched at it with his finger. "They're boats to the Aran Islands! From some town out in the country. That's his company! He owns it!"

"What makes you think that?" Rory asked. "This doesn't say anything about a Seamus O'Leary."

"I was down at the pub with some of the guys from Gaillimh Boat Tours—"

"You *what?*"

"—and one of their friends heard my predicament and said he knew of this company owned by Seamus O'Leary. He took me back to the office and gave me this!" Aidan snatched the brochure back to dance around the room like a deranged mental patient.

"Since when do you go drinking with strangers?" Rory demanded.

"There are a lot of things you don't know about me, bro!" Aidan grabbed Rosie by the hands and dragged her about with him. She only hesitated for a moment before a smile escaped her lips and the old Rosie was back, strutting her stuff around the sitting room. Seeing her happy again, I couldn't stifle the grin that was growing on my face. We'd gotten a break at last!

But when I finally looked at Rory, he looked downright petulant. I wanted to touch his arm, comfort him somehow, but the roller coaster that had been his emotions lately, crashing into my first, failed *I love you*, made me keep my hands to myself.

Aran Ferry Ltd. didn't have a website and nobody answered the hundred times Aidan called the number on the brochure that evening or the next morning.

"We'll just have to go there," Aidan said with finality.

"If they're not answering, they're probably closed," Rory said darkly.

"I'm not going to argue with you," Aidan said, leaving the room. "I'm going. You can come if you want."

I couldn't tell whether Rory's face held more anger or hurt, but I knew he would be going, too, so I scurried off to get a jacket.

Rossaveal was a forty-minute bus ride from the city. The smooth promenade of Galway City gave way to rocky coast, and the drive followed the angry waves for much of the way. Rain and wind buffeted the windows, but I eagerly watched, with my nose pressed up against the cold glass, each of the houses we passed, perched on the rocks down near the ocean. What a spectacular place to live!

Before I knew it, Rosie was getting up from beside me to follow Aidan and Rory down the aisle. I scrambled after them, but there was no need to rush. The bus emptied completely here.

"Thanks for the heads up," I muttered, joining my travel buddies by one of those big black *bruscar* trash cans. Directly across the street from the bus stop was the ocean. A long line of big, white boats was moored there, each beside a long concrete walkway that stretched into the water, creating a neat line of bobbing ferries. That's where most people from the bus, and others emptying around us, were heading now. There was an awful lot of people, bundled against the rain, walking away from the boats, too.

"What *are* the Aran Islands?" Rosie asked.

But there was no time to chat. Aidan was on a mission. "There!" He pointed through the misting rain to a cluster of tiny buildings a short way off.

"The Aran Islands are a bunch of trailers?" Rosie grabbed my hand and pulled me along as the boys started toward the little trailers perched on bricks. Colorful signs adorned them, each claiming to be cheaper than the next. Aidan looked over his shoulder, probably to see what was taking us so long, and excitement lit up his features despite the wind and the rain. Rory followed suit, but he looked downright nauseous. The contrast made my heart twist.

The trailers were arranged in a small semicircle around a patio of asphalt. People milled around under umbrellas and slick raincoats. Aidan and Rory stopped here, their eyes on the trailer in the middle. There was a big blue sign that had white block letters on it, shiny from the rain.

*Aran Ferry Ltd.*

My heart began thumping. Was this it? Was I ready for this? Sure, Seamus O'Leary wasn't my dad. But I'd heard enough about him last summer to feel as though I knew him … and I wasn't sure I liked what I knew.

The wonderful, weathered face of Mrs. O'Leary swam before my eyes and for once I remembered her fondly. Not for the terror she'd brought into my life but for the gentle, kind old woman she'd been. Seamus O'Leary had kept her captive on land for many years. I gulped and grabbed Rosie's hand as Aidan exchanged a look with Rory and marched confidently toward the open door of the gleaming white trailer.

A wide sliding door was open, a set of concrete blocks acting as stairs up into it. A tiny counter was the only furniture in the room, every available surface plastered with photos of what I assumed were the Aran Islands. They looked gorgeous. Wild and barren, like a world from long ago.

The trailer was similarly barren. There was nobody in here.

Aidan turned to Rory, who merely shrugged.

"Oh, well—"

"Hi, there! Sorry to keep ye waiting," a middle-aged man said, ducking into the trailer and hurrying behind the counter. "Here for a refund?"

"Uh, no, we don't have tickets," Aidan said.

"Oh, well we're not selling today. Only refunds. The boats won't be going out, there's a monster afloat."

*Kelpies*, I thought immediately. *Or Teran.*

"We, uh, we're actually here to see Seamus O'Leary," Aidan said, a smirk pulling the side of his face into an expectant look.

"Jesus, Seamus O'Leary?" The man folded his arms over his chest and rested a palm against his scruffy cheek. "Can't say I've seen him in, oh, two years. Or three was it? No it was two. It was the summer Dan O'Brien Ferries moved out here. Terrible competition, and Seamus wanted out. Don't know where he ended up after that." The more he talked, the greater the despair on Aidan's face became.

"Are you kidding me?" he finally snapped.

The man looked at him like he'd been bitten.

"He, uh, he doesn't own Aran Ferry anymore?" Rory asked gently, glancing at the look on his brother's face.

"Oh, no, lad. I bought the boats and the name off him going on two years ago. My lady wasn't terribly thrilled, but a job's a job, you know? And I got me more boats than the average Irishman. She wanted a man with land, but, eh, I say, if we've got the boats, we got more land than anyone in Ireland. Just so happens our land's underwater." He chuckled, a tiny whistle accompanying it.

Rosie and I both began to laugh, but Aidan turned and stalked out of the trailer without another word. Rory watched him go, a look on his face that almost resembled hurt, but I knew it had more to do with his little brother's pain than the disappointment of the false lead.

"Thanks anyway," I said with a smile, trying to keep the mood light as the man raised his eyebrows at Aidan's exit.

"Tell your wife a guy with a boat is a huge commodity in the U.S.," Rosie said. "Better than a farmer by far!"

The man chuckled. "Arah, she thinks it's an unsteady way to make a living. And sure on days like these, nobody can go out and I have to eat before I come home or I won't be eating at all!"

Rory politely said good-bye and headed for the door.

"Don't let her beat you up about it too badly, it's a noble profession!" Rosie called over her shoulder when we were at the door. "Once you find your calling in life, you stick to it!"

Her eyes were glistening a little too much for comfort. *Time to go.* I clutched her wrist and pulled her out of the trailer with a friendly wave at the boatman. We *had* to get to the bottom of this emotional well of hers and stop it up. Maybe a second pregnancy test would convince her not to worry. The only problem was even *I* was afraid of a second pregnancy test. What if it confirmed that the first was wrong?

Aidan was standing behind the bus stop we'd been at only minutes before. His hands were shoved into his jeans and his face was pointed away from us, but I could feel the murderous vibe emanating from him like the waves crashing against the shore just across the road. His hair was plastered to his ears in angry little spikes.

The rain was a mist, as if someone was spraying us with a spray bottle rather than the heavens opening up. Rory looked up at the bus schedule taped to the single post that marked the bus stop. The schedule was no more than a piece of paper, and it was splattered with rain, making the tiny times difficult to read. "Hey, do you know what time the next bus for Galway arrives?" he asked in Aidan's general direction.

"I don't give a shit," was the reply.

Three pairs of eyebrows shot up as Aidan wheeled around and crossed the street toward the water.

Rory shot a glance at Rosie and me then followed his brother. "Okay, I know that was a disappointment but—"

"Disappointment? We're at the end of the line! I'm running out of ideas!" He kicked at a rock, sending it sailing into the water. The ferries were tilting dangerously in the waves, and I was no seafaring woman, but I definitely wouldn't take a boat out in that. Twirling around, I saw Aidan heading back toward the bus stop, as if he was trying to lose us. But Rory wouldn't let that happen. He got right up in Aidan's face.

Maybe giving them some space was the best course of action here. I stepped over to Rosie, who stood a few feet away, trying to pretend she wasn't watching the spectacle. *Stop poking the bear, Rory,* I thought miserably.

No such luck.

"What is your problem?" Rory demanded.

"What's my problem? What's *your* problem? Why the hell aren't you pissed? We just came all the way out here for nothing! Absolutely nothing!" Aidan walked in figure-eights, his hands fisted at his sides.

"Who cares? Why is this so important to you?"

"Are you kidding me? He's our freaking *dad*, Rory!" Only he didn't say "freaking." Things were going south fast.

"So what?" Rory spat. "We already have a dad. And a mom. And like a billion brothers and sisters."

"That's not our dad," Aidan said darkly.

For a very long moment I thought Rory was going to hit him. Rory's jaw was ticking and his fingers were twitching. "Don't talk like that about the man who raised us," Rory said in a dangerously smooth voice. "We'll find Seamus O'Leary some day, but you need to chill the hell out."

"I will not *chill out!*" Aidan yelled, slamming a fist into the red bus stop pole, which vibrated from the impact, and the wet tape on the schedule gave way. As we gaped at Aidan, gentle, sweet Aidan, the wet paper fluttered to the ground and came to a stop at his feet. A group of tourists speaking another language moved warily away from him.

"I'm running out of time," Aidan growled, his nostrils flared.

"Time for what?" Rory demanded.

"It doesn't matter," Aidan said. I couldn't be sure because of the rain, but Aidan's flashing eyes didn't look dry.

*Is he crying?*

"Aido, get a grip," Rory said. He looked so sad, I almost reached out to comfort him, but that would hardly make a difference. It's not like he wanted my comfort. Or my love.

"Why don't you care?" Aidan snarled. "Why don't you care about any of this? This is bullshit!" He whirled around and kicked the *bruscar* trash can, which skidded across the concrete with an angry scrape and toppled over, spilling a splash of paper onto the sidewalk.

Rory's mouth hung open. Aidan's chest was heaving and when he saw Rory looking at him, he stalked away toward the water.

This time, Rory didn't follow.

# *Na hÉireannaigh Troda*
## FIGHTING IRISH

MRS. O'LEARY VISITED ME IN MY DREAMS THAT night. She hadn't visited me since I'd gotten to Ireland, and I liked it that way. But after my fond memory of her that day, she returned. My mistake. I was standing on the jetty, late at night, as the waves roiled about in preparation for a storm. I strained my eyes against the water pounding me from above, looking, looking, looking for something in the water.

A hunched form would walk out of the ocean, wringing a drenched housecoat with one hand, holding something leathery and brown in the other. I ran to the beach and waited for the figure to meet me there. Lia O'Leary. Sometimes she was young, or how I imagined she would have looked when she was young. And sometimes she was just as I remembered her from last summer.

This night, she stopped when she saw me, the waves still racing for her ankles and surrounding them before falling back only to regroup and come at her again. Never giving up. Never letting go.

She never spoke. She would hold out the sealskin, imploring me to take it with just one burning, soul-searching look. It was like she could take my soul in her hands and break it open, freeing all the pain and questions and fear with just a look.

Most nights I woke up at that point, sweating into a wet patch in my sheets. But this night, I reached my shaking hand out and took the skin.

At the same time I grasped it, another hand grasped mine. I whirled around and found myself gazing up at Rory. Then he gently removed my hand from the sealskin.

Mrs. O'Leary turned and retreated into the waves, and Rory followed.

*No!*

It took me a few long moments to realize my eyes were open. And I wasn't on the beach. I sat up on my elbows and squinted into the dark. A light was flashing from the nightstand beside the bed. Rory's room. Roz's snores. My phone.

It felt comforting to feel something so familiar in my palm. I had a missed call and voicemail. There were only a handful of people who called me at all, and one of them was snoring next to me.

Dad's voice sounded tired and a tiny bit confused as he began speaking after the short *beep*.

"Hi, Cora. I got your message. Thanks for calling."

*Could he sound more businesslike?*

"Um, I, uh, I did know about the lawsuit. So you can go ahead and toss that letter. They sent one to every possible place I could see it. There's probably one at my regular Starbucks." A small, bitter laugh. "Um, I … Well, as you seem to know, yes, there is a bit of legal action happening with Fullington Factory. But this is a conversation I'd rather not have with your answering machine. Call me back."

I thought it was over, when I heard him clear his throat into the phone. "And, um, maybe call over the weekend. We have free long distance then."

*Right, because we're scrimpers and savers now.*

My thumb was about to press *delete* when my father's voice said very quickly, "If your mother answers, just ask for me. I, uh, haven't had the chance to get her up to speed on everything."

*Click.* The message ended and my stomach plummeted.

Placing my phone back on the nightstand, I took a deep breath, trying to break through the wall that seemed to have closed off my throat. So my dad was being sued. People got sued all the time, right? But why hadn't he told my mom?

My parents' marriage was something I'd always taken for granted. Lying to them, as a united front, was something I'd done on multiple occasions. I did it earlier this week to take this trip. But lying to my mother *for* my dad? That wasn't okay. It made me downright nervous.

I swung my legs out of the bed, massaging my tense throat with my fingertips, and tiptoed around the dark room. I desperately needed some water.

My toe came into contact with the dresser, and I bit my lip to keep from cussing. I didn't want to wake Rosie up. Who knew how many perfectly restful nights she had left?

And when on earth had my life starting spinning so far off its axis? Right. Last year. The Summer that Changed Everything.

Slipping out the door, I padded quietly down the hall. If the boys were asleep, I could sneak into the kitchenette in the sitting room and get a cup, then fill it up in the bathroom sink.

But when I pressed my ear to the sitting room door to gauge their stages of REM, it wasn't snores I heard.

"You just coughed for like ten minutes straight!" Rory was hissing behind the closed door.

"So? It's ridiculously damp in this country," Aidan hissed back.

My hand drifted away from the doorknob. I wasn't about to interrupt a sibling squabble, especially not after Aidan's tantrum that afternoon. But my ear didn't budge. It was stuck to that door as if it was oozing super glue.

"You look pale," Rory said, even quieter this time.

Somebody scoffed. "Thanks for the interest in my beauty regimen, but I haven't exactly had the time to go sunbathing," Aidan said. The sarcasm in his voice wasn't playful. It was toxic.

"Oh, so busy, are you?" Rory spat back. "Video games taking up a lot of your time?"

"Shut up."

"Just cut the crap, Aidan! Do you promise me that if I called Mom right now she would *not* tell me that you've had a relapse?"

My heart thudded around like someone had kicked a bass drum. *Relapse?* Aidan had been sick? When?

"Oh, yeah, please, go call mom like we're seven years old again," Aidan snarled.

"We weren't seven at the same time," Rory mumbled.

"As if she wouldn't have told you the first time you called her. As if she wouldn't be on a plane right this very second. God, what happened to my brother—the one that was my best friend?"

There was a painful silence. I almost pulled away, because there were tears pricking at my irises, but one of the boys cleared his throat.

"You swear to God you're not lying to me?" Rory said in a husky voice that made every inch of me yearn to hold him. My pinky twitched. I'd made a promise to Rory once. A pinky promise.

"You know what, screw this. I'd rather not sleep at all than sleep in this room." The sound of shuffling made me dart down the hall back to Rory's room. I peeked out the door as a dark figure flew out of the sitting room and down the hall. The front door slammed a few moments later.

Why was Aidan acting like this? Soft-spoken, demure Aidan. I thought I'd known him. But I didn't know him, I realized with a jolt. None of us did. We didn't even know his real name.

## *Deartháracha agus Dheirfiúracha*
## BROTHERS & SISTERS

I FEEL LIKE I'M LOSING HIM, AND I DON'T KNOW how to get him back," Rory said softly. We were stretched out across the back of a bus en route to the home of one of the older O'Brien boys. Aidan hadn't wanted to go, but Mrs. O'Brien had alerted the family of his presence in Ireland and Rory had arranged this so he couldn't escape it. "I don't know what else to do."

Of course I didn't know how to corral the spiraling Aidan, but a few ideas came to mind. Like not fighting with him. Maybe telling him about the incident with the sealskin and the red welt that *still* graced Rory's hand. But instead I was silent.

Why was it so difficult for me to talk to him? The roller coaster he'd had me on was growing difficult, that was true. But whenever I saw his eyes, the jagged ice lodged in my chest started to melt. Whenever he talked to me, I remembered the Rory from last summer. But the minute I did anything, like, say, utter the words *I love you*, he put on this mask that made him look like a stranger. Was he really done with me? Just like that? Maybe it was because I'd flown across the ocean like a madwoman. Or because I'd kept this secret from him for a whole year. With that in mind, was it so difficult to understand he might really be done with me? I could almost believe it, until he opened up his heart once again, just like he was now. I wanted off this roller coaster, but I wasn't sure I'd like what I found if I did manage to get off.

"I'm hoping this mini family reunion will remind him who his real family is," Rory said. "And, you know, take his mind off 'Operation Selkie.'"

I nodded absently. It was the most I could manage. Rosie and Aidan were embroiled in a conversation on the other side of me, and I hadn't seen Rory or Aidan speak a word to each other all morning. Rory had called in to ask off work and when he told Aidan some of their siblings wanted to see him, Aidan looked … well … indifferent.

I didn't say anything about what I'd overheard the night before. And nobody mentioned it. I found myself watching Aidan, analyzing whether he looked thinner than usual or paler, wondering what illness he'd gone through in childhood. But the truth was, I hadn't *really* known him before this summer, barely acknowledged him last summer. I wouldn't be able to tell if he really was keeping something from Rory. But, surely, Mrs. O'Brien would have mentioned something that important when Rory called. As if I didn't have enough on my proverbial plate already. God, I *really* needed to stop eavesdropping.

Once Rory became quiet, I was able to pop in my headphones and drift to sleep, so the trip there was quick enough. The family lived outside Dublin, and his brother, a tall, friendly guy with a weird American-Irish twist of an accent like Declan's, picked us up from the station in a sleek BMW. He was … nothing like Rory and Aidan. He looked a bit like Declan, but he had the clinical air of a doctor or lawyer.

"Conor's a professor at DIT," Rory explained, as we got out of the car in front of a neat, semi-detached house with the sounds of children coming from the back. As Rory shut the car door, I saw the hand still sporting an angry red welt where the sealskin had latched on to him with an unnatural vigor. I didn't have time to dwell on it, as we moved toward the house and a Jack Russell greeted us at the door along with a little girl with blond pigtails. She said nothing, just stuck a finger in her mouth and attached herself to Conor's leg.

"Hey, Lucy," Rory said, squatting to talk to the girl on her level. "Can I have a hug?"

She appeared to consider it but decided against it, burying her face in Conor's slacks and hanging on like a barnacle as he moved to the kitchen.

"Well at least Ben likes me," Rory said, scooping up the terrier.

My senses tingled as we entered the room. It was full of more vivacity than any room in my house had ever seen.

The sliding glass door was wide open, and kids playing in the grass in the back yard came running when the guests arrived. Two women and a man who looked vaguely like Conor sat at the table, one of the women absently rocking a baby who cooed at her mother's face contentedly. Lucy detached herself and ran over to an even smaller little girl as if to say to us, "Look what I have!" A cousin? A sister? The five-year-old's gloating poked a tiny hole in my gut, leaking the air I needed to think clearly.

When I was little it was common for me to wish I had a sibling. Someone to play with, to fight with, to unite with against Mom and Dad. Didn't every kid, regardless of siblings, dream of having a twin? But I'd never felt the yearning so strongly as when I stepped into that room.

Everyone moved at once, as though we were the conductor's baton starting an orchestra. They shouted, they laughed, they hugged, and not just Aidan and Rory. I found myself trying not to squish the baby as her mother, Kathleen, introduced herself with a hug and a peck on each cheek.

"Man, you guys are like bunnies," Rosie said as the two little girls brushed past her to run out of the room.

As Conor plied us with drinks, Kathleen ushered me to the table and plopped down beside me with the baby.

"This is Áine," she said, pronouncing the name "Oawn-ya."

Rosie made a whimpering sound beside me.

Rory, arms free of dog, swooped in and plucked Áine out of her mother's arms. She squealed excitedly.

*Oh be still, my beating heart.*

The baby touched his face with a slimy hand.

"Ick!" he moaned dramatically, while wiping his face with his sleeve.

"Rory, Rory, I won my football match yesterday." An older boy was bouncing in the periphery, trying to pull Rory's attention away from the baby.

"Leave him alone, Kevin," somebody moaned.

"Did Declan not come with ye?" Kathleen asked.

It was then that I realized Aidan wasn't paying attention.

"No, he said something about your kids being awful," Rory replied with a smile. He pressed the briefest of kisses to the peach fuzz on Áine's head.

"Ah, well, he's got us there," Kathleen said, and the table erupted in snickers.

Aidan sat at the end of the table, staring out the glass doors at the kids who had retreated outside with the Jack Russell when the newcomers were deemed not all that exciting—I couldn't blame them. But Aidan wasn't watching them with amusement, or even fondness. He looked like he didn't see them at all.

After setting two glasses of Coke between Rosie and me, Conor sat down next to Aidan.

My ears pricked up like a dog's when I heard Aidan say, "Hey, Conor, have you ever heard of the selkie myth?"

I froze.

*What in the hell was he doing?*

I couldn't exactly join in their conversation with the laughs and jokes going on at this end of the table, but I could eavesdrop and one look at Rory told me he was doing the same. His eyes were shooting not daggers but full-size spears at his little brother.

Conor had a bit of a confused look on his face. "Of course I have. It came out of the Orkney Islands in Scotland and permeated a lot of the coastal communities in Ireland. But similar concepts exist in lots of other folklore around the world. Why do you ask?"

"Just wondering," Aidan said nonchalantly. "Saw a painting about it the other day at the market." He looked up and saw Rory—who looked murderous—rolled his eyes, and looked away.

Oh God, was I going to experience the first instance of selkie fratricide?

"It's a really interesting one," Conor went on, oblivious to the tension in the room. "It's all about seals that turn into people and come ashore. They think it arose from a great number of people, undereducated and unable to swim, living in close proximity to the ocean. In some cases, even making their living on the ocean, fishing. An astounding number of fishermen in early coastal communities couldn't swim."

*Yeah, that's a plausible theory. Or maybe it arose from seals turning into people.*

"This terror of the deep was passed down and, like many stories, gained mythological status. Myth often sprouts from an attempt to explain events that people can't understand."

"What does the myth say about how long selkies live?" Aidan asked.

Conor looked utterly perplexed. Even a sister-in-law looked over in confusion.

Conor mumbled, "Uh, I don't think I've ever—"

"I mean, do they live as long as humans? Or as long as seals? Or are they on some completely different time frame—"

Suddenly, there was a baby in his lap.

Rory was standing over him, eyes holding the starkest warning I'd ever seen in them.

Aidan's mouth dropped shut, but his eyes narrowed as he obediently stuck an arm around Áine.

"Hey, Conor, will you show me that bike you bought?" Rory said.

"Absolutely!" As Conor got up, chatting away with Rory, a brief storm passed over Aidan's features, the very sea itself roiling in his eyes.

I turned back to my end of the table, but everybody had been watching the baby drop with interest. Everybody but Rosie, who wasn't sitting next to me anymore.

She was standing outside, her back to the house. Ben the Jack Russell stood next to her as though the two were engaged in a deep conversation.

"Roz?" I said, stepping around toys in the grass to stand beside her.

Tears were pouring down her face.

"What the—" I darted forward and turned around so we were face to face, placing my arms on her heaving shoulders. The Jack Russell cocked his head, unhappy to be left out of the embrace. A glance over her shoulder told me we'd gone as yet unnoticed by the people in the kitchen. "What's the matter?" I hissed.

"I don't want that, Cora," she wailed with a wave behind her. I'm sure she meant to wave toward the house, but she'd actually indicated the neighbors', who I'm sure had a fine family.

"Shhh," I said, hoping she'd take the reprimand as soothing and not my desperate attempt to make her lower her voice. "Don't want what?" We could *not* have a meltdown right now. I needed to get a handle on this situation ASAP.

"The kids. The babies. I'm not ready! I'm not ready!"

"Rosie, I know. It's okay. Everything's going to be okay. The test was negative. If you don't believe it, we can get another one."

"I had to take a test yesterday, too. It was just spelling, but I'm not a good speller." My eyes landed on Kevin, the football braggart.

*Dear God alive, if he asks what kind of test, I'll evaporate.*

"I don't think I spelled subtract good because Martin says there's a *t* at the end and even though I don't think there's a *t* at the end, Martin is smarter than me."

"Oh, I'm sure he's not." *What the hell?* I had bigger problems than mending an eight-year-old's self-esteem!

"Is she crying?" Kevin asked, scrunching his nose up in disgust.

"No," I said.

"Why is her face wet?" he asked.

"She's having trouble with her allergies."

"What's allergies?"

"Go ask Martin how to spell it," I snapped.

Rosie snorted. "They're so annoying! I couldn't take it."

"You're annoying!" Kevin shot back.

"No you are!" Rosie snapped.

*Oh dear Santa of the Chemists, our lord and savior, do* not *make this girl a mother.*

"Hey, Kevin, could you show me how to use that?" I pointed to a long, wooden thing on the ground that looked like a deformed baseball bat. Anything to get him to walk away.

"It's a hurley," he said.

"Can you spell it?" Rosie said with a watery smirk.

"Rosario, you are fighting with an eight-year-old!" I hissed at her.

"I'm seven," Kevin stated proudly.

"Show me how to use the hurley, Kevin," I said, as if commanding a dog. Ben must have thought the same, because he ran over and chomped his teeth down on the stick as Kevin tried to lift it. The dog went with him. Perfect. A distraction.

I whirled back around to my deteriorating best friend. "Rosie, you need to a get a grip. I know you're freaked out. But the test was negative. Trust. The test. If you haven't noticed, Aidan is falling apart in there. He almost divulged Operation Selkie to all those people. I cannot handle two of you going off the deep end!"

Rosie snorted.

"No pun intended. Now, we're going to go back inside and you're going to sit there and pull it together."

"You do this!" Kevin shouted. "You're not watching!"

"Scratch that, we're going to stay here and you're going to *stand* there and pull it together."

Kevin swung the hurley around, whacking what looked like a baseball with the flat end of it. The dog went soaring after it, knocking little Lucy down in the process.

Feeling eyes on me, I looked at Rosie. She was smiling through her drying tears.

"What?" I demanded.

"When did you become the strong one?"

I shrugged. I certainly didn't feel like the strong one.

Rory came out the back door then, Áine back in his arms. The mere sight of him made me feel like the *weakest* one. Kathleen leaned in the doorway and watched as Rory kicked a soccer ball toward one of the older boys, Áine bouncing gleefully in his arms.

I'd daydreamed about having a sister before. But what I hadn't realized as a kid, which struck me as painfully truthful now, was exactly how close I'd come to having a sister.

Watching Rory interact with his brothers' kids twisted and knocked my heart like it was a fleshy Bop-It.

# *Tá Sé Casta*
## IT'S COMPLICATED

THERE WERE ONLY TWO OTHER PEOPLE I KNEW who were practiced in living for years in the wake of a tragedy. Well, Mrs. O'Leary was nowhere to be found, so I didn't count her anymore. I couldn't afford to lose the other two. Or for them to lose each other.

On the bus ride back, Rory and Aidan were both asleep next to strangers, having refused to sit next to each other. Rosie's head was nodding beside me, but there was a gentle hum from chatter around the bus, and I needed to do this.

The phone rang four times, the threat of the answering machine looming, when Dad finally picked up.

"Hello?" he said desperately. "Cora? Is that you?"

I gulped. "Yeah."

His breath was loud in the phone. "I'm sorry you had

to find out about the lawsuit that way."

"Why are you being s—" I glanced nervously around at the closely packed passengers. "What's it about?"

"It's just about money. They're claiming breach of contract."

"Did you do it?" I asked.

"It's not that simple," he said.

"Oh, I'm sorry, please dumb it down for me."

"Look, Cora, the rainbow shoelace days are over. We've been trying to match that success ever since the fad died. But that's easier said than done."

I sucked in a breath, and my stomach sank at the idea that Fullington Factory had been flailing for who knew how long, and I hadn't so much as noticed. I'd always made fun of my dad for the rainbow shoelaces. Little did I realize they were feeding and clothing me.

"Cora, I don't want to do this over the phone. Nothing will happen for a long time yet. The courts are slow as molasses. We'll talk about it when you get home."

*That's fine with me.*

But there was one thing that *wasn't* fine with me. If he thought he was getting out of this conversation just like that, he was wrong.

"Did you tell Mom?"

The sharp intake of breath on the other end may have been imaginary, but it was unlikely. "Not yet."

"Why not?" I asked.

"It's complicated."

"Funny how you can work that into such a short conversation twice. God, if you're about to be sued for all you're worth, maybe you should stop making international calls." I regretted it almost immediately, but I hung up then. Worrying about my parents' marriage sat firmly down upon my fear for Rosie which was already lying on top of concern for Aidan's recent behavior. Not to mention that Rory was seriously not handling any of it very well. Or rather, not at all. He was acting like he wanted it all to disappear without a trace.

The next morning Rory was donning a hunter-green hoodie and was about to leave the house when I woke up. Aidan was hunched over a laptop and didn't even look up when I walked into the living room.

"Hey, I'm going to walk Rex," Rory said. "Do you want to come?"

So completely taken aback, I didn't respond.

"Aido's going to be hoarded up in here all day Googling Seamus O'Learys and selkies, and he's even talking about going to the county council, so there probably won't be much to do around here."

"Yes," I finally managed. "I'd love to."

"Me too!" Rosie appeared in the doorway just as I turned.

I could have slapped her then, even some evil-eye action would probably have done the trick, but the memory of how distraught she was yesterday kept me from saying—or eyeing—anything.

Eyre Square was just yards away from the apartment, and Rex was small enough that he was exhausted by the time we got there. Rory had brought along a maroon blanket that said "Galway" in the middle, and he spread it out on the grass in an empty corner of the grassy expanse intersected by walkways. The advantage of Rosie being here was that I had to sit closer to Rory for us all to fit on the blanket. As soon as we plopped down and Rex climbed into Rory's lap, Rosie starting eyeing a group of kids with an inordinate number of dreads. They had a thin line stretched in the air between two trees and were taking turns attempting to walk it.

"I wanna try! Cora?" She pulled off her hoodie and jumped up.

I eyed Rory. "I think I'm going to pass for now."

"C'mon, Manchester! Live a little!" Rosie bellowed, but she was already scampering away.

She didn't know that sitting here, alone, with Rory, was the kind of living I liked. And quite exhilarating enough.

Rory was petting Rex, but was watching the tall girl with braids carefully walk the rope. "I wish Aidan would have come," he said absently.

"Yeah," I said, completely unhelpfully.

"I've missed him a lot this past year. But he's—he's like somebody else entirely now."

*Isn't it funny how people can be so different than you remember? So distant?* That's what I was thinking, but what I was *feeling* was the familiar sight of Rory sitting close to me, his skin so near I wanted to reach out and touch it.

"I just don't know what's going through that kid's head. Definitely not our family. It's like he doesn't give a shit about our parents or our brothers and sisters anymore. I don't think he played with the kids once at Conor's."

There was a moment of silence before I forced myself to say, "I—uh, I overheard something the other night."

Rory closed his eyes for a moment, then nodded. "I know he's hiding something from me, and I really thought that was it, but it can't be. Mum would have told me."

"Um, what, exactly?"

Rory expelled a long breath before answering. "When Aidan was like, four, he was really sick."

I felt a little nauseous myself thinking of sweet Aidan, who had recently become angry Aidan, being sick Aidan. "With what?"

"Well he had Hodgkin's lymphoma, but he recovered really well. He went through treatment, and for the first couple of years they said he was in 'remission,' but after eight, nine, ten years, you know, you're just a regular kid again."

*Holy shit.* "I-I had no idea." Poor Aidan. As I sat there thinking about this revelation, my eyes fell on Rory's hand, which still bore a red welt from our experiment with the sealskin. "Out of curiosity, did you tell Aidan about that?" I pointed at the spot, which was much smaller than it originally had been.

"No." Rory wasn't looking at me.

"Oh ... are ... are you going to?"

"No."

Of course not. And if Aidan never found his sealskin, he'd never know. There was a silence in which I pondered how my next question would be received. The obvious answer was: not well, but for some reason my vapid brain said, *Full steam ahead!* "Did they not—um…I mean, when Aidan was going through treatment, nobody noticed, like, what he is?"

A storm of emotions took over Rory's face and his nostrils flared as he took my free hand and pressed it against his chest, not very gently. "I'm a human being, Cora."

Despite my every fiber celebrating the feeling of Rory's heartbeat beneath my palm, the look on his face said Operation Selkie—any part of it—was *not* up for discussion. I gulped and whispered, "I'm sorry. I'm glad he's well." Rory let my hand slip away and I pulled it back and clutched it to my chest as if I could keep the feeling of him in my fingertips forever.

"Well, when you guys first got here, I thought he'd relapsed or something. He's been coughing a lot and he looks skinny—I mean, skinnier than usual. He's always been scrawny, but…Anyway, that's not possible, because A, Mum would not have let him out of the house, let alone the state, and never the country, if he'd had a relapse, and B, if he'd somehow managed to squeeze through the cracks, she'd have told me on the phone, or, you know, called Interpol by now."

A smile grew on my face at the very believable prospect of Mrs. O'Brien directing a herd of police officers. "I've noticed him coughing, too."

"Yeah, he said he had mono in May, which Conor actually mentioned when we were at his house. There's not a lot that gets away from the family rumor mill."

"Well maybe you should call your mom, just in case," I said.

Rory shrugged. "Probably should. But what would I say? 'Oh, hey, Mum. I just noticed Aidan was acting really strange and hostile as we searched for our birth parents who may or may not be an animal and a murderer, so I was wondering if you knew anything about that.'"

"True. That might not go over so great."

"Probably not. But I do know Aidan went on some dates with this girl from his class who I happen to know likes a *lot* of boys in their class, so I wouldn't be surprised if she gave him mono."

I snorted. "Sure, blame the girl."

"Trust me, Aidan wasn't exactly a ladies' man when I was living at home, and I don't think he's become some ladykiller in my absence. He'd need my help for that."

Laughing out loud, I felt at once like I was hanging out with the boy who had become my best friend last summer. It felt so incredibly wonderful.

"Do you still swim?" I asked on a whim.

He nodded. "Yeah, the university has a pool. The ocean's too cold for it most of the year. But not for a lot of very old Irish men and women who swim religiously all winter. They just strip down—"

"Oh no. Speedos?"

"Exactly!" He laughed and I joined in.

"What's so funny?" Rosie came back to us, a little out of breath. Rex jumped up and sniffed around her shoes.

"Cora thinks I'm not charming," Rory said with a definition-of-charming smile.

"That's not what I said!" I shrieked.

"Hey! You guys weren't even watching my performance! I stayed on for, like, five whole seconds!"

"You'll have to practice to reach circus standards," I said.

"Oh, sounds like a challenge, doesn't it?" Rory laughed.

"No, I was merely—"

"Go! Go, Cora! You can*not* insult me and then not prove your superiority!"

"Do it!"

"Go!

"C'mon!"

"Learn to live a little!"

With a smirk I jumped up and stomped over to those rope-walkers.

"You want a go?" a boy asked as I eyed the rope, which looked *much* thinner close up.

"Why not?" I stepped up onto it, testing my weight before lifting my other foot and placing it in front of me.

*Shit.* This was hard; the rope was swaying furiously. I tried to bring my left foot around in front of the right, but the rope dipped to the left and I went flying.

Right into Rory's arms.

He was laughing hysterically as he swooped me away from the rope and planted me back on my feet. "That was like less than two seconds, Cora," he said.

That didn't matter. I'd take falling into Rory's arms over joining the circus any day.

# *Cailín na Gaillimhe*
## GALWAY GIRL

WHEN WE LEFT THE APARTMENT TO GO OUT that night, I was still riding the high of the feeling of his arms around me. Sure I was still on the Rory roller coaster, but it had crested a very high hill this afternoon. I just hoped this was the end of the ride—that a dip or a twist wasn't just around the bend.

"We can't go to The Quays," Rory, in a Captain America t-shirt, shouted over our boisterous friends— Niamh and Niall rounded out our usual group. "I told them I was sick!"

After the week I was having, I'd been starting to feel that way, too. Until this morning in Rory's arms. My worry-induced nausea had started to give way, but as we stumbled down the street, I was beginning to feel a nerves-induced nausea. There was one cure that I knew would take my mind off *everything*. The Irish cure.

"Fine! Don't get your boxers in a bunch!" Rosie shouted. She didn't need alcohol to bring her to life—and she wasn't going to get any while I was on might-be-pregnant-lady watch. She was in her element, her worries forgotten as she strutted down the street in a short black dress, shiny gold shoes clicking on the stones. She was clutching Aidan's arm, but Rosario Balducci was never on the arm of a boy. The boy was on *her* arm.

Niamh had offered to dress Rosie and me "Irish style." If she was going on a night out with Rory in a short, sparkly dress, I sure as hell couldn't be left behind. I didn't exactly feel comfortable with so much of my thighs baring their goose bumps to the world, but standing next to Niamh in one of my knee-length dresses would have been even more embarrassing. She'd put me in a blue, one-shouldered, sequined dress of hers and a pair of her stilettoes, but before we left the apartment, I'd swapped my own one-inch heels for her monstrosities.

Aidan was leading the way up Shop Street, Niamh on his other arm. Niall was trying to talk to me about football, by which I think he meant soccer, but I was mostly ignoring him.

The street here was crowded with young people already drunk and others in official-looking black windbreakers that bore the names of different bars and clubs. They wielded stamps, battling each other for every drunken person's hand.

"Coyote's! Free shot for everybody who comes with me!" one guy yelled.

"No," Rory said sharply as Rosie held her arm out to be stamped.

"I'll go anywhere but there."

"Like The Quays?" I said, as innocently as possible.

He mock-glared back at me.

"Let's go there!" Rosie squealed, pointing excitedly at a line along the street perpendicular to Shop Street. People in various states of inebriation were crowded on a dirty red floor mat that had been pulled out onto the sidewalk.

"Carbon," Aidan chirped. He was swaying slightly, and I hadn't seen him drink anything yet, but he didn't appear to be sober.

I studied the back of my hand and the trail of stamps that looped around and up the inside of my arm. I definitely didn't have a Carbon stamp, but nobody stuck around to hear my assessment. I tottered after them about as gracefully as a baby horse learning to walk.

Carbon was loud and dark with flashing lights, but we'd waited long enough to leave the apartment that it was already rather crowded. Rosie dragged Aidan out to the dance floor, so I followed the others to the bar.

As Rory ordered a beer, Niamh placed her perfect little hand on his arm and whispered something in his ear. The feline that erupted inside me was not of the itty bitty kitty kind. It was a tiger. This tiger knew: whatever was going on with Aidan or Rosie or even Rory himself, Cora Manchester was still *desperately* head over heels for Rory O'Brien. And it was time she did something about it.

"Rory—"

He didn't even hear me over the bass. "Hey, we're going to go sit down!" he shouted toward my ear as he handed something fruity-looking to Niamh.

"Okay, I'll be right there," I said, but he was already moving away toward the suspicious-looking booths in the corner.

Niall had his beer now, too, and was turned away from me talking to a girl on his left. Apparently she was more interested in football than I could even pretend.

"One—" The bartender moved away as if I hadn't spoken.

Great, by the time I got a drink, Rory and Niamh would be married.

I lifted a finger in the air as the bartender moved back toward me. He raised his eyebrows as if to say, *Yes?*

"Oh, one—"

"One Sex on the Beach and two Bulmer's!"

I turned to see who had spoken over me and was met with a pair of really big boobs.

*So that's how this works.* I looked down at my chest, more bare than I was used to in this dress, and pulled it down a little farther. Then I stood as tall as I could manage and leaned forward.

A few minutes later, Vodka Red Bull in hand, I warily stumbled toward the booths. There were a lot of stairs and very few lights. My insides felt like sweet, fluffy cotton candy as my eyes took in Rory sitting at the booth. Alone.

But then again, that could've been the Red Bull.

I surreptitiously pulled the neckline of the dress down a bit farther and slid in beside him. Hey, it'd worked for my drink. Before he even looked at me or my boobs, he was talking. "I don't think it's working."

Following his line of sight, I found Aidan dancing with a stranger. Nearby, Rosie was entangled with a dark-haired boy.

"It's like he doesn't even care about our family anymore," Rory muttered. It was quieter here, but I could still only just make out his words. He was still pouting over his unsuccessful bid to erase Operation Selkie from Aidan's mind.

I took a large swig of my Vodka Red Bull and winced. *Note to self: This is disgusting.* "Can I ask you something?" I said, testing the boundaries of how emotionally deep you could really get in a nightclub.

"Shoot."

"You don't seem to care whether we find Mr. O'Leary or not."

He sighed and I turned to look at him. "I guess I don't," he said simply.

"You don't want to talk to him?"

Rory shrugged. "I guess I don't want to find somebody who doesn't want to be found. I mean, if he cared, he would have found us, right? He's the one that knew where we were. All this time."

It was true. If Seamus O'Leary was still alive he hadn't sought out his sons who'd been living exactly where he'd left them years and years ago. It was the first time I thought of Rory and Aidan as being abandoned. Like Mrs. O'Leary, like Mr. Hall, Seamus had abandoned his sons, too.

"I never thought of it that way," I admitted. "I guess Aidan doesn't, either." And I wanted to agree with Rory, but in my head, I was siding with Aidan. *What do you want him to do?* I wanted to ask. *Forget it entirely? Forget your real parents? Ignore the evidence of some seriously magical shit in this world?* I knew now that he wasn't too keen on Seamus O'Leary, but that didn't mean he had to forget *everything*. Besides, why would he want to forget it all? And how? I'd tried to forget it for nearly a year and had failed miserably. And I wasn't even a … you know.

Here they stood, two brothers on opposite ends of the world. One wanted to embrace the past, know everything, find everything, and the other seemed … disinterested. Like he wanted to throw away the gift. Or was it a curse?

"Would you give it all up if you could? Forget it all and never talk about it ever again?"

His eyes found mine. The colorful strobe lights from the dance floor flashed and faded, rendering his eyes foreign and unfamiliar. Those weren't Rory's eyes.

"Would you willingly forget Mrs. O'Leary and Mr. O'Leary and everything you've been told?" I pressed.

"Gladly."

My eyes were starting to have trouble looking at the table, which was rocking to and fro by the time Aidan suggested we move to another club. Turns out Niamh was quite funny. I hadn't had a chance to talk to Rory any more with the arrival of her and Niall, but it was easier to laugh in my current state than try and unravel Rory's complex emotions.

"Go get her, please!" Niamh demanded, pointing toward the dance floor. "I want to go to Electric Garden."

Laughter and really unattractive snorts erupted from my nose as I noticed Rosie on the dance floor. Or, rather, near the dance floor. She was pressed up against the wall, locking lips with the dark-haired stranger she'd been with earlier.

As Niamh and the others laughed, I made my way over to the couple. They weren't the only ones entangled in public displays of saliva. *That's dangerous*, I thought, inching carefully around another couple, who were dancing dangerously as their tongues flashed.

"Rosie?" I tapped her on the shoulder. There was no reaction. "Rosie!" I bellowed, punching her in the arm.

They pulled apart with a disgusting squelch and Rosie yelped. "Ow!"

"We're moving on to another place!" I yelled over the music.

"Oh, okay!" She turned to her new friend. "Sorry, I'm leaving."

"Aw, no," he said. His eyes were squinting as if the beer had rendered him hard of sight. "Stay a while. You can come home with me."

*Oh God.* I didn't normally get involved in Rosie's exploits, but I couldn't very well let her run off with a guy in her current state of the gods' indecision. Not to mention this was a stranger in a foreign country.

"Come on, we can make this last all night," he said with a gross grin. "Come home with me."

My mouth was open to step in and proceed to cock-block, but Rosie smiled then. Not her flirty smile, but her condescending smile.

"Not tonight, stranger," she said, ducking under his arm braced on the wall. She winked at him and pulled me, a shocked shell of a human, to our friends who were standing near the door.

"When did you become the responsible one?" I said.

She smiled at me—not her flirty smile or her condescending smile, but her sad one. I could write a book on the many smiles of Rosario Balducci. As she shrugged, a feeling of motherly pride welled up inside me.

"Let's go to the beach!" Niamh screeched.

"If you want to freeze to death," Niall said. "This isn't Greece."

"Stop being such a downer!" And with that, the lamest of arguments, we were dashing—actually dashing—across the town. Down Shop Street and across the bridge over the Corrib, I shuffled as fast as I could. How Rosie and Niamh were beating me in three-inch heels was a mystery for the ages.

With a quick left, the walkway turned gravelly and the wind picked up and we had to pick our way over grass and bramble. There was a short concrete wall, and Rory extended a hand to help me hop down. Then the grass gave way to sand and rock and the night wind infused my lungs with a life-giving air I'd never felt before.

Or maybe that was the vodka.

Regardless, it was so beautiful that I forgot myself. I forgot that I was nineteen and really self-conscious and nursing a zit on my nose. Everything evaporated and I felt gorgeous. The mountains and the ocean seeped into my pores and I was gorgeous and beautiful and ancient as the earth. You couldn't feel anything but stunning in these waters.

Yeah, that was definitely the vodka.

I kicked off my heels and ran for the waves, hopping and groaning as my feet met painful rocks. I waded into the freezing waves as the rest of the group excitedly followed suit. But I didn't stop.

"You're gonna drown!" somebody yelled from farther back.

Instead of a terrorizing fear, a thought like I'd never felt before surged up inside me. What if I did? What if I waded just a few steps farther out and let the undertow take me? I'd know at long last what it had been like for my sister. *My sister.* It wasn't often, if ever, that I said or thought those words. Maybe I'd have a sister at long last if I just took a few more steps ...

"Cora."

Or would Rory save me? Would he kick off this weird scorn for his true identity and dive into the waves and save me? *Maybe I should do it just to remind him of his affinity for the water. The way he used to swim in the ocean every morning and I'd watch ...*

"Cora, come back."

Without even looking, I stepped backward toward the shore, the voice bringing me back like a gravitational pull.

When I turned and waded all the way back to the shore, Rory was standing there, and we were completely and utterly alone.

# *Siúlóid i mBróga Duine Eile*
## A WALK IN SOMEONE ELSE'S SHOES

I KNOW I'M THE ONE THAT TAUGHT YOU TO SWIM, but I wouldn't exactly trust my teaching skills in this water," he said.

"Where did everybody go?" I asked.

He shrugged and looked around. Our so-called friends were already halfway down the walkway back to the city. "Niamh said something about Róisín Dubh."

My feet were soaked and now caked in sand.

"You want to walk?" he asked, gesturing toward the dark, empty beach. My chest ached with the implications. I couldn't manage anything other than a weak nod. Folding my arms against the cold, I followed suit as he walked slowly toward the waves.

He stopped when he was up to his ankles and walked away from the city. My heart was in my throat, rendering me completely speechless. How many times I'd dreamed of walking happily down the beach with Rory, like we had last summer. But so much had changed this past year. Or not changed at all. Things had just come bobbing to the surface after I'd kept them buried, for a whole year, deep beneath the water. Where they belonged.

"Full moon," I said, pointing to the sky.

"Nearly. I don't think it's quite full yet."

"That means spring tide's coming."

A smile lit up his face. "You remembered."

I nodded, but some sort of emotion strangled my throat, and any response turned into a gulp. What I wanted to say was, "You have your sealskin, you have spring tide, you could become a seal!" But that would only depress and mess with this romantic vibe we had going.

*Keep it normal, Cora.*

After several quiet moments, Rory stopped walking and chuckled.

"What?" I asked, my face echoing his smile.

"This isn't nearly as fun as I thought it'd be," he said. "It's extremely cold. And the rocks hurt my feet."

I laughed outright, the wind swallowing the sound in a second. "It really is like walking on Legos."

He spun around. "Let's head back toward civilization."

*No!* Civilization involved people and I wanted to be the only person in Rory's orbit right now. Or ever again. I'd wear Lego shoes for the rest of my life if Rory was by my side.

In the distance, the lights of Galway twinkled like Christmas lights. Rory hopped up on the low wall and extended a hand to help me up.

As my feet made contact with concrete, I slapped a hand to my forehead.

"My shoes!"

If I had any notion of re-seducing Rory O'Brien that evening, it was blown to smithereens by the twenty-minute search for my shoes that followed.

"Weren't we closer to here?" Rory called, as I drifted farther down the beach.

"I don't know!" I wailed, digging my toes through the sand like little bulldozers. If only I hadn't picked black shoes!

"Maybe the tide came in to where they were," Rory suggested.

"The tide?" I repeated helplessly.

"It's okay," Rory called. "We can buy you some new ones tomorrow."

Dropping to my hands and knees, I sifted sand through my fingers. The beach was far too dark to find them now. By morning, they'd be a pointless present for a mermaid.

"Cora, I think they're gone," Rory said, crouching beside me.

I pouted and looked up.

He was holding his Nike tennis shoes out to me. "My feet smell like tulips, I promise." When I made no movement to take them he went on, "It's a really interesting thing, actually. I've been the subject of a lot of studies. Some days it's more like a sunflower or a Gerbera Daisy, but today it's tulips."

Some emotion was punching the backs of my eyes, begging to be released in the form of tears. "Why do you know so much about flowers?" I asked with a sniffle.

"Don't question the finer points of my intelligence." He hopped up onto the concrete wall and dropped his shoes in the grass, hand outstretched to help me up. "Come on!"

"My feet are all sandy," I said, grabbing his hand and climbing onto the wall.

"So are mine," Rory replied. "But I bet yours smell like roses."

As soon as he released my hand, I wiped my nose and slipped my sandy feet into his shoes. It was uncomfortable and itchy but my heart was trying to convince my brain I was walking on clouds. Rory started toward the glittering town, and I followed after one last look of longing toward the beach that ate my shoes.

"Why do I mess everything up?" I groaned.

"You don't," Rory soothed. He didn't hold my hand, but he got close enough that I waited for skin contact with nervous anticipation.

"Yes I do. I failed to get into any good university, I'm in community college, have to pick a major in the fall, and have no drive to do anything at all," I recited. "Which part of that spells success?"

"There's a difference between wild success and messing things up," Rory said. "You know you can just *be*. That's a success in itself."

He stopped walking and looked at me for a moment. At least he looked toward me. It was too dark for me to see his eyes. "Come here," he said, grabbing my hand and pulling me down the path.

It wound around a squat building with a playground and a bevy of sleeping swans, then came to a tiny harbor where Rory stopped. All kinds of boats were tied up to old, massive, rusty metal rings coming out of the ground at our feet.

"What am I looking at?" I asked.

Rory pointed at a garish boat painted orange and brown and red and white, all chipping. It looked ancient, a "For Sale" sign hanging on the mast. And, most importantly, due to the changing tides, it was nearly level with the ground right now, maybe a half foot below.

"What about it?" I asked. "Are you going to buy a boat?"

Rory laughed. "Some day, yes. Right now, no."

With a short run, he leaped the foot gap and landed on the boat's dusty wooden floorboards with a *thud*.

"Rory!" I hissed.

"What?" he hissed back, mocking me.

"That's trespassing!"

"I don't see any cops, do you?"

I stood on the precipice, like a superhero about to leap from one building to the next. In the gap the waves crashed against the seawall below. Green moss covered the side, evidence of the ever-changing tide.

"Come on!"

I shook my head.

"If you even make me come get you …"

*Ain't no mountain high enough, isn't that how it goes?* I backed up a few feet then ran as fast as my stumpy legs could carry me. Arms and legs flailing helplessly, I launched through the air and landed like a sack of potatoes on top of Rory.

He laughed as we tumbled to the wooden floor.

"Ow!" I yelped.

Every part of me tingled as I lay, flush against him. My limbs hurt from the impact but my chest was aching for a completely different reason. I longed to move my arm, to feel my skin brush against his. But I was afraid to break the spell.

The temptation not to move overwhelmed me, but Rory rolled us upright and got to his feet, steadying himself against the gentle rocking of the floor.

"Since when did you become a trespasser?" I said, dusting my aching knees off. "If I remember correctly, the last time I tried to get you to trespass, you were very against it."

He raised his eyebrows. Apparently the night had held more significance for me than him.

"The Ritzes' pool?" I prompted.

His face cracked into a grin. Maybe it did mean something to him, after all. "The Ritzes could've sued me out of house and home. But whoever owns this boat isn't doing as well, by the look of it. Might not be able to afford a lawyer." Bending over, he picked up a large chunk of paint that was lying, completely unattached, to the wood. "A Ritz boat would never look like this!" His imitation of Mrs. Ritzes' airy voice was impeccable. He flicked the chunk of paint and it landed on a pile of ratty ropes coiled in a corner.

I giggled and clutched a rusty pole next to me. The vodka already had my knees quaking, but put a boat under them, and there was a good chance I wouldn't be upright for much longer.

"Maybe we should buy it!" I suggested happily. "Or just sail away right now. I guess, technically, that would make us pirates. We could sail away and find Mrs. O'Leary."

His face clouded over.

I was going for playfulness, but I should have known not to go there. The vodka made me forgetful. I needed to backtrack. Fast.

"I've missed this," I blurted out. The clouds in his face cleared as his face fell back in surprise. "I've missed *you*," I clarified. "Rory, I—"

"Hey!"

We both jumped and spun around.

"Hey, you there!"

"Oh, shit!" Rory yelped.

"Get off there! That's trespassing!"

Laughing, Rory grabbed my hand and pulled me back toward the seawall. I didn't have time to look for the boat security guard because I was suddenly aware of the way back. The wall was about a half-foot above the side of the boat.

Rory let go of my hand and clamored onto the side of the boat, jumping swiftly to the seawall. But his legs were long and lithe—mine were like baby trees in a vodka wind.

"Cora, come on!" he hissed. "The guy's coming over here!"

"Get the hell off my boat!"

Clutching a dirty rope that led up to the seawall, I climbed nervously onto the side of the boat, which dipped and swayed as though it was trying to buck me off itself. The gap between the boat and the wall was suddenly a gigantic chasm with alligators and sharks and mermen and who-knows-what below.

"I can't!" I hissed, terror climbing up my throat.

Rory glanced behind him at some threat I couldn't see over the wall. "Staying is not exactly an option right now!"

With a deep breath, I launched myself off the boat, but the wuss in me didn't let go of the rope. I never stood a chance.

"Rory!" I gasped, fingers scratching at the stone seawall, hanging onto the rope for this dear, messed up life. "Help!"

In retrospect, I must have been hollering like a loon, because there was a smile very close to the surface of Rory's face. He bent and grabbed hold of both my hands, tearing them from the security of the rope. In one swift movement, he'd hauled me over the side and I landed on my knees.

Just in time to see a *very* angry, *very* large middle-aged man lumbering toward us.

"Come on!" Rory shouted. Pulling me to my feet, he sprinted toward the ocean, and I had no choice but to keep up, clomping behind him in shoes much too large for my feet.

"You godforsaken—"

Whatever we were, I couldn't hear over the scream of the wind in my ears. Rory leapt over a short stone wall and pulled me down among a sea of boats overturned on the rocky beach. I'd seen this place before, from across the river.

Rory crouched behind a bright yellow, right-side-up boat with a tiny wheelhouse, tall enough to hide us both, and pulled me down beside him. "Ow," he sighed, rubbing his toes. I only then remembered he was barefoot.

His chest was heaving as he smiled at me. "That was a stupid idea, Cora," he whispered.

"That was *your* idea!" I yelped.

"Shh!" He pressed a hand over my mouth and listened. There was no noise but the crash of the waves and the far-off tangle of music from the lively pubs around the town. My lips gloried in his touch, even if his hand did kind of smell like old paint.

Rory peeked over the edge of the boat then plopped back down, releasing my mouth. "He's gone," he said with a smirk.

Everything inside of me came rushing out at once: the breath I was holding, the vodka vapors, the strangled emotions for Rory. I felt light as I sat there on the pointy rocks, my hip so close to Rory, I could feel his jeans against my thighs.

"What is this place?" I asked. The boat across from us was an upturned black and white rowboat with broken oars. There was a neatly stacked pile of rusty lobster cages beside it.

"It's the boat graveyard," Rory said simply.

"Huh?"

"Mum used to bring Aidan and I here when we visited Galway when we were little to see all the old boats. It's the boat graveyard."

"They come here to die?"

Rory shrugged. "Sometimes you see people out here painting them, so I guess they're not dying so much as ... finding new life." He jerked his thumb over his shoulder. "I saw an old guy painting this one a couple weeks ago." He leaned over me to look at the front of the boat. "Her name's Talulla."

I didn't look where he was pointing. His face was too close to mine, and it stole my breath away. It felt familiar and terribly foreign all at once.

*Just do it.* He was close enough that the slightest movement on my part would end in a kiss. The tiniest movement—but it took the greatest willpower. *Live a little, Manchester.* I'd just flown halfway around the world—okay not quite that far, but across an ocean—to tell this boy how I really felt and so far we'd gotten nowhere. He looked at me and this time, I didn't stop to read his eyes. I leaned forward and brushed his lips with mine.

He pulled away.

Embarrassment flooded me. That was it. He'd just denied me outright. No ambiguous roller coaster or hints. That was clear as day. He didn't want me anymore. I needed to run. I needed to get up and run to the airport. I jumped to my feet, or rather, his shoes, but they wouldn't carry me away. Tears were springing to the surface and if I didn't talk right now, they'd spill over in a storm of epic proportions.

"One minute you're sweet and caring and just like the Rory I was with last summer and then the next minute you're cold and distant!" My voice was trembling like a magnitude-eight earthquake. "I don't know how to act around you! It's like a roller coaster! Why are you doing this? Why are you messing with me like this?"

"Me?" he bellowed.

"Yes you! Why are you acting like this?"

"Why?" he said loudly, something sinister flashing across his face as he jumped to his bare feet. "Why do you think?"

"I don't know!" I wailed, crying in earnest now.

"You broke my heart, Cora!"

Despite the seagulls and the crashing waves, deafening silence pounded in my eardrums. There was something shimmery behind his beautiful brown eyes and for a second that took years to occur, he looked as though he was going to cry.

"I loved you!" he shouted. "You were the first girl I ever loved. The first I ever said 'I love you' to. I loved you so much and you just disappeared! You stopped emailing, stopped talking to me, didn't even tell me why! It was like I meant nothing to you! You meant *everything* to me!"

I was melting.

I had ceased to exist.

Where was I? Wherever I was, it was spinning.

"You just dumped me like I meant nothing! I loved you more than I'd ever loved anyone!" He expelled a breath laced with tremors. "You ..." He shrugged, his nostrils flaring, and his voice deflated. "You broke my heart."

In the time it took for a gull to cry overhead, I was standing alone beside a bright yellow boat in someone else's shoes.

# *Faoistin Chonamara*
# CONNEMARA'S CONFESSION

Y OU GROW UP, LOCKING YOUR HEART AWAY INTO a carefully constructed box so that boys won't break it. Everyone warns you, teaches you the charms and spells to ward off heartbreak. To recognize the signs and traits of a likely perpetrator. But nobody ever tells you that you, too, hold the power to break hearts.

I was an empty shell where Cora Manchester used to live. The lonely piece left behind when a crustacean makes a change of address. Said crustaceans from Galway Bay were on sale at the weekend market, which was thriving on a Sunday in the shadow of the ancient church.

Ambling around aimlessly, back in my trusty jeans, I was trying to make myself feel like less of a total bitch. It wasn't working.

"Sun's splitting the rocks today, i'n't?"

I looked warily around. An old man sitting on a low stone wall beside a booth selling leather bracelets was looking straight at me.

*Is he talking to me?*

"Yeah, I'm talking to you," he said, pointing a shaky finger at me.

*Holy shit.* "Uh, yeah, it is," I said.

I must have look confused because he said then, "That means it's hot."

"Oh, yeah, of course," I agreed. Not St. Louis hot, but it sure was giving the air-condition-less Irish town a challenge. I suddenly recognized this man as the one who'd given Aidan and I a ridiculously creepy lecture on the first lynching. *Martin something?*

"Do you remember summer last year?" he asked.

I shook my head.

"It was on a Thursday!" His laugh was a bellow from his belly and drew looks from curious tourists who wanted in on the laugh. I smiled weakly, wishing I had the boys with me for translation.

They, their hangovers, and Rosie had been fast asleep when I woke up this morning, so I'd wandered down Shop Street aimlessly. Really only trying to put as much distance between Rory O'Brien and myself as possible. I wanted to be alone with my thoughts, be around strangers whose mere presence could keep the tears away, to wander, unrecognized. Irony was my worst enemy.

"Anyway, come with me."

My head snapped up. "What?"

A proud smile crept across his face. "Somebody wants to see you. Yer a Yank, aren't you? I think you're the one. Ya better be, if I'm ta'get my pint. Follow me."

He got up and shuffled through the crowd, leaving me too stunned to do anything but follow him. Was it the smartest move? Probably not. But he was moving at quite a pace for an older gentleman, leaving me little room to ask questions. Like maybe, "Are you an ax murderer?" I probably wouldn't have understood his reply, anyway.

*No dark alleys, old man.* At the first sight of a creepy van, I'd run.

But there was no van and no dark alley. His destination was a pub. The pub that backed up to the market, a wide array of beer kegs stacked in a complicated maze outside the door.

"Are we allowed to go in this door?" I mumbled to absolutely no one. Because Martin had already walked into the dim place, leaving me hesitating on a heavy-duty floor mat.

I followed reluctantly, and the bartender and his one customer on a stool at the bar eyed me suspiciously.

"I'm twenty-one!" I yelped, guilt flooding me.

The pair of men gave me a look that questioned my sanity. People had been doing that a lot lately.

*Get a grip, Cora, you're not in Kansas anymore.*

"Hey, Yank!"

That had to be me. After casting a cautious glance at the bartender, I moved toward the dark mahogany booth Martin was standing beside. When I reached him, my mouth open to demand an explanation, he moved aside, revealing somebody else in the booth.

Colm Vesey, to be exact.

"M-Mr. Vesey?" I stuttered.

"Call me Colm." He looked up at me with a harried look, then glanced behind me as though hoping I wasn't the grand total of what he could expect.

"Where are the boys?" he asked. His hand tightened around the pint of Guinness sitting in front of him, with the signature white foam at the top. The glass also said "Guinness" along the side, probably for noobs like me.

"They're … not with me. I … I can go get them," I offered, half-hoping he'd deny it since I hadn't yet faced Rory since last night.

"No, no, it might be better this way," Colm said. He gestured for me to sit as Martin moved away without a word. He drifted to the bar and pounded his fist on the shiny wood there.

The bartender groaned and went to pull a pint without conferring with Martin.

Colm chuckled, but the mirth didn't reach his eyes. "Hope he didn't scare ya too bad." He sipped his pint and I wondered briefly what it tasted like. It couldn't be good.

I glanced back at Martin who now held a Guinness, too. "How … how did he know who I was?"

Colm snorted, wiping his mouth with the back of his hand. "Doesn't everybody know Martin? I just ran into him in the market this mornin', but I've never had a trip to Galway without meeting Martin in the street. Anyway, I've been here all weekend looking for you lot. But when I saw you out in the market, I chickened out. Had to send him to get you and take myself to get one of these in me before I could talk." He held up his glass to indicate where he'd found his courage. "All I had to pay Martin was a pint."

I would have laughed if I wasn't so worried about why Colm had hunted us down in Galway City. Had he found out something new about Seamus? After all this time? Had Seamus heard we were here and tried to run away?

"What brings you to Galway?" I asked, as pleasantly as possible.

"I am not quite sure myself," Colm said. "Guilt, mostly. And memories of Lia, God rest her soul."

*He came all the way to Galway because he wanted to reminisce about Mrs. O'Leary?*

"She … she was a wonderful woman," I said.

"Tell me, girl. Did she die?"

Rory had told him she died last summer. Was it a case of an old man not remembering everything or …

"Or did she leave?" he said, as if to challenge my honesty.

I gulped. "She left," I nearly whispered.

He nodded. Slowly. Like Mrs. O'Leary had done countless times last summer. It was like I was sitting across the booth from a ghost.

A loud *thwack* made me jump as a slick pint flew across the table. Martin stood, his own pint in hand, and watched the one he'd just released come to a halt in front of me.

"For the Yank," he said.

*Shit.* It was a Guinness. I couldn't very well turn down a gift, could I? Beer wasn't something I enjoyed, so this was going to be awkward.

"Thanks." I smiled, feeling the fakery on my cheeks like bright paint.

"Ever had Guinness?" Martin asked.

I shook my head.

"Then go on, give her a try!"

*Shit shit shit. That was your out. You should have said,* Of course I've had Guinness, *and changed the subject back to Mrs. O'Leary.* As if that topic was any safer.

"Go on," Martin repeated. All eyes were on me, even the bartender's and the red-streaked pair belonging to the patron at the bar.

"Okay," I squeaked. I lifted the glass and tilted it, keeping my lips so close only a trickle of bitter brown ale or lager or whatever the heck it was made it into my mouth.

"Go on! Give her a real chance!" Martin shouted, tipping the end of my glass up.

I panicked, taking in a gasp of air—and a whole lot of beer. Almost as much came back out as I spluttered, my tongue writhing at the bitterness.

"It tastes like a tree!" I cried.

The four men burst into laughter, Colm included, as I wiped my face with my sleeve.

"Have you tasted a tree?" Martin asked. "My, ye Yanks are strange."

"No, but it's how I imagine a liquefied tree would taste," I muttered.

"Ah here! I paid you, Martin," Colm said, shooing the man away with a leathery hand. "Leave us be!"

"Arah here, I'm going," Martin said, shuffling away. "Just let me know if you need a refill," he added with a wink at me.

I pushed the wet glass across the table. "You can have that," I murmured.

Colm made a sound that nearly resembled a laugh but fell short. "Thank you for coming with that crazy lout over there. What is your name?"

"Cora," I said obediently.

"Well, Cora, I imagine you're familiar with the O'Learys. And the O'Brien boys, of course."

I nodded.

"There's something I need to tell them. Only, you showed up first, and if you could just tell them what I have to say, it would make it much easier on an old man."

"Okay," I murmured.

"I loved Lia O'Leary, God rest her soul, a great deal."

*Whoa. Okay. So we're diving right in.*

"A great, great deal," he added, as if that would clarify anything.

*So did I*, I thought. I couldn't say it out loud, because it still hurt so very much when she visited my dreams. My nightmares. In each one, she was the embodiment of everything I feared. But I wanted to remember her by all the conversations we'd shared in Oyster Beach.

"That alone is the reason I came to say this. It may be an old man's folly. But I loved that woman, God rest her soul, and she would want them to know."

"Know what?" I asked.

"Not that it was my place to love her," he barreled on as if I hadn't spoken. There was some sort of internal war going on inside him, and I wasn't sure he was going to tell me what he came here to say. "I promised him I would never tell a soul. But I've been sitting, thinking about it ever since you lot came to my house. They remind me of her. The boys. They have her eyes."

Now that was something that people just said. I knew that. It was a cliché. But in that moment, I thought, just maybe they *did* have her eyes.

"I thought so many times this week of how we used to be," Colm said, his mind a million miles away. "Those days in Oyster Beach are some of my fondest memories.

For the first time, I saw Colm as a young man. He had a bulbous nose now, but in his youth it may have been part of an attractive face. My mind's eye smoothed his weathered skin into a youthful, freckled mien. Was Colm Vesey jealous of Seamus O'Leary?

"Colm, what do you want the boys to know?"

"That I lied," he said simply.

I sucked in a sharp breath. "You know where Seamus is?" I asked eagerly.

"No, I don't, that much was the truth. But I *do* know where that sealskin is."

"Where is it?"

"I made a promise to a dear friend many years ago. Forgive an old man for his loyalty. There comes a time when loyalty is a crime, and this was one of those times. The skin is on Inis Mór with Kieran Browne."

# *Dhá Bronntanais Déas*
## TWO NICE SURPRISES

I KNOW WHERE IT IS!" I BURST INTO THE apartment, excited to be the bearer of good news for once. "Aidan was right—he was lying!"

"What was I right about?"

"Who was lying?"

Rory and Aidan were sitting in the living room with Niall and Niamh. Since I was yelling like a banshee, all eyes were, of course, on me.

"Colm Vesey—I just ran into him. You were right; he wasn't being truthful. He didn't 'get rid' of the … the thing you're looking for. It's on Inis Mór."

"What?" Aidan spluttered, jumping up.

"Are you talking about yer da?" Niamh asked, looking around, perplexed.

"Some guy told ye he was going to get rid of yer da?"

Niall asked.

Aidan looked like he was only barely containing his urge to jump for joy. He even let out an uncharacteristic fist pump. My eyes fell on Rory. He was looking at me like I'd just handed him the mangled remains of his favorite bicycle.

*Shit.* How could I be so stupid? I was so wrapped up in solving the mystery, being the bearer of the news, that I'd forgotten there was no way Rory would be happy about this. He'd give it all up if he could, he'd said it himself. *Stupid, stupid Cora.*

"Well, let's go!" Aidan shouted, skipping around the couch to grab my shoulders. "Let's go!"

"There's only one more boat today. We wouldn't be able to go there and get back tonight."

"Then we'll spend the night there!" Aidan said.

"What is Inis Mór?" I asked quietly.

"Don't be stupid." I wasn't quite sure whether Rory was talking to me or Aidan, but considering I'd smashed his heart into smithereens, I figured I deserved worse than that.

"I don't care what your problem is," Aidan yelled at Rory, "I'm going!"

"We'll go tomorrow," Rory said quietly, evenly.

An awkward silence descended upon the room, Niamh and Niall looking at each other with raised eyebrows. They both got up and mumbled excuses before leaving the room, and I was considering doing the same when an almighty shriek rose from the hall.

Rosie burst into the room, a smile plastered on her face. But I was pretty sure she hadn't heard my news, so I wasn't sure what the smile—

"I'm noooot pregnaaaaant!"

Aidan and Rory looked at her, horrorstruck. This, of course, didn't faze her and she twirled and shrieked and pranced around the room, even hopping up onto the couch to do the running man.

"I'm freeeee!"

"Congrats, Roz," I mumbled.

Noticing our stunned expressions, she paused. "Did I interrupt something?"

"Uh, Cora just told us she knows where the third sealskin is."

"Okay, okay, that's equally as cool, I guess. Wahoooo!" Rosie commenced bouncing about and Aidan jumped up onto the couch with her, grabbed her hands, and proceeded to holler like a madman.

My friends were really losing it. But, for the time being, two thirds seemed ecstatic at the moment, and that was a blessing given how the emotions had been roiling so far this trip. There was just one left who was still down. And that was partly because of me.

I couldn't very well control the whole his-mom-is-a-mythical-creature part of his sadness, but the broken heart part was entirely my fault. We needed to talk.

# Rothair Browne
## BROWNE'S BIKES

THE NEXT MORNING WAS BLUSTERY SO WE SAT ON the lower level of the boat which was, mercifully, completely closed in except for the constant stream of people opening the door to go up top for the open view. Our row was comprised of four teenagers, one half grumpy, one half elated.

Turns out Inis Mór is one of the islands in the trio that makes up the Aran Islands, off the coast of County Galway. It is the biggest of the islands with a whopping population of like 900, but also a booming tourist spot by the looks of the other boat passengers—and much like the rest of what I'd seen of Ireland. We'd gotten the bus to Rossaveal again, this time buying ferry tickets from the company that used to be Seamus O'Leary's.

The ride across the bay or channel or whatever it was

was extremely choppy, making the boat bob from side to side, so that we got a full view of the scary big waves out the windows every three seconds. Luckily, Rosie was chattering in my ear about Luke—who was suddenly attractive again now that she was for sure *not* carrying his child—and it gave me something to focus on. Rory was silent and Aidan had his faced pressed up against the window. Just when I thought I was going to have to interrupt her to lose my breakfast, people started standing.

I hadn't even noticed the boat had stopped, because it was still tipping this way and that, but within moments the gangplank had been extended and people were pulling out cameras.

"It's gorgeous!" Rosie shrieked, a hand over her eyes as she stepped onto the long pier.

While the mainland had been warm—the apartment downright hot—it was almost chilly out here. This last tiny bastion of Irish land before the wild Atlantic, it was absolutely whipped by the sea wind, big waves hitting its shoreline—which was a large ratio of its land. But Rosie was right; it was beautiful.

The rocky coastline was buffeted by waves, but the land beyond it was as green as you'd expect from the Emerald Isle. There was a small cluster of brightly painted buildings at the end of the pier that seemed to be a town. Armed with the new info from Colm Vesey, Aidan had failed to find any mention of a Kieran Browne but did find a "Browne's Bikes" on the internet last night. Aside from "Inis Mór," there was no address, but judging by the size of the place, that wouldn't be a problem.

"This is it," Aidan said, excitedly tugging at the straps of his camo backpack.

"Five is the last ferry back," Rory warned angrily. "We can't miss it."

"Yeah, whatever."

"Okay, selkie boy, let's go!" Rosie chirped, looping her arm around Aidan's.

I fell into step beside Rory as we made our way toward the small town. There were a few cars on the streets and vans waiting to lug tourists around, but more than both, there were bikes. Bikes were everywhere.

"It's pretty," I said.

Rory just grunted. After all, it was a lame attempt at conversation with the boy whose heart I'd broken, for which I'd failed to apologize yet. That needed to happen pronto. If only I could get the monologue in my head to come out of my mouth. *I'm so sorry, Rory. I loved you, I never wanted to hurt you. But I was stupid and more afraid of getting hurt than hurting someone else. I'm so sorry. I never stopped thinking about you. I still love you.* None of the words were particularly long or complicated, so why oh *why* couldn't I just say it?

After a few moments, I noticed he kept checking his phone. Rosie peeked over her shoulder then and noticed our silence. I shrugged.

"Expecting a call?" she asked Rory.

He looked at her for a moment then nodded. "I called my parents yesterday. Nobody answered. Waiting for them to call back."

Nothing came out of my mouth but inside I felt warm. He'd

listened to me, followed my advice. Now if only I could get my apology out, maybe we could be talking about this to each other rather than having Rosie as an interpreter.

"There it is!" Aidan shouted, pointing ahead a few yards to a blue storefront that sported more bikes than one could possibly imagine would fit on this tiny island. A cluster of people were in front paying a guy wearing a "Browne's Bikes" t-shirt.

"I think I'm gonna go buy a water bottle," Rory said, stopping. He stuck a thumb over his shoulder and then turned to go back to a tiny shop we'd passed at the end of the pier.

This was a tad off because Rory and Aidan were each wearing a backpack stuffed full of chips—er, crisps—and sodas we'd bought before leaving Galway. But this was obviously difficult for him and he needed a moment.

Rosie and Aidan turned, frowning, and seeing him walk off, Rosie looked pointedly at Aidan and then nodded toward Rory's back.

Aidan rolled his eyes.

"We'll wait for you there, just go," she said.

Aidan let out an almighty sigh before shuffling off after him.

"What was that about?" I asked.

Rosie looped her arm around mine and kept walking toward the bike shop. "I told him he needed to freaking make up with his brother. Those two have been at each other's throats for too long. They're brothers!"

I smiled. Maybe she wouldn't make such a terrible mother after all. One day. Definitely not until she outgrew her "Ramen makes a great

breakfast meal" phase. Or her "Vitamins are for old men" phase. Or …
well, a lot of her phases.

"Let's go find us some sea lion skin!" she chirped.

"Shhhh!" I hissed, eyeing the group with the salesman. "And it's
seals," I corrected in a whisper. "There's a difference."

"Whatever."

A tiny bell dinged above our heads as Rosie led the way into the
shop.

"Hello!" a man behind the counter bellowed. He looked up from
the counter as we approached, revealing a pair of piercing green eyes.
Those eyes made me think he'd probably been quite attractive when he
was, you know, not ancient. He was quite obviously old but solid, with
broad shoulders and carefully kept white hair. He wore what I was
coming to recognize as the old Irish man's uniform: plain brown pants,
a crisp white shirt, and a pair of suspenders with a tweed-looking jacket.
"What a beautiful day you have here on the island. Looking to rent
bikes?"

"Um, actually, we're looking for Kieran Browne."

The man quirked his head, surprised. "Oh," he said. "I'm afraid
Kieran isn't here right now. Are you friends of the family?"

"Yep," Rosie said cheerily.

"Well, Patrick is here," the man said, gesturing out the front
window of the shop. The salesman stood alone now, hands behind his
back, awaiting fresh customers. "He's owned the shop for a while now,
so Kieran doesn't spend much time up here."

"Ah." Rosie poked at her lip with a finger. How would we explain knowing the old man but not the son?

Just then, I heard Aidan's booming "Hello!" muffled by the front windows. I turned to see him and Rory greeted by the salesman.

"I think our friends want to speak with Kieran," Rosie said hesitantly, glancing over her shoulder at the boys.

"Our friends are inside," Aidan was saying to the salesman, pointing toward us.

When I turned back around, the old man was halfway through the door to the back of the building.

"Oh—" Rosie muttered, turning around, too.

"Just going to see if I can find him around the place," the old man shouted over his shoulder. "Back in a moment."

The bell over the door tinkled as Aidan said brightly, "Hey, guys!"

"Hey," Rosie said. In the background behind her words, I could hear rapid whispering in the back room. I couldn't tell if it was thickly accented English or Irish. "We asked for Kieran," Rosie went on. "The guy that was working the desk went to look for him. The business belongs to his son now or something."

"Great!" Aidan smiled broadly.

I watched Rory carefully. He wasn't smiling exactly, but he didn't look quite so grumpy as earlier.

A woman who looked to be somewhere in her thirties appeared from the back then. She looked sort of harried, though she quickly composed herself and smiled at us.

"Hi," she said.

"I don't think you're Kieran," Aidan said.

She laughed, short and nervous. "No, no. I'm Deirdre. I was told you wanted to speak with him, though. I was going to suggest ye take some of our bikes over to the café, and I'll call Kieran and ask him to meet you there."

We all looked at each other. Was this place just desperate for customers?

"You don't have to pay for the bikes," the woman said quickly. "He's just over on the other side of the island, and I don't bet ye've a car on the island."

Aidan finally shrugged and said, "Okay."

"Wonderful." The woman grabbed a pamphlet from a stack on the counter and scribbled on it. "If you go outside, Patrick will help ye find bikes. Follow this route." She handed the paper to Aidan, who was obviously the ringleader of our weird group, and headed for the door.

"That was weird," Rosie muttered.

"No kidding. Do you think Kieran's going to try to run or something?" Aidan asked.

I snorted. "It's an island. He won't get very far."

"You don't think that guy was Kieran, do you?" Rosie asked quietly.

"Huh." I thought for a moment. It could have been, but Kieran Browne didn't have a reason to ignore us, two random American girls. "No, I don't think so. I think we just took him by surprise by being so suspicious and creepy. What would a bunch of young Americans want with an old man who lives on a remote island off the coast of western Ireland?"

"Good point."

The woman was speaking to the sales guy in Irish, and then retreated inside as he helped us pick out bikes. It was mildly embarrassing as he tried two bikes with me before he found one that was sufficiently short, but as soon as we were all outfitted like true tourists, Aidan started spouting directions.

"This way!" He pedaled off without even looking to see if we were following.

The land was bumpy and the road seemed to be crumbling into gravel, but it was beautiful. Barren, rocky, but beautiful.

Before we'd left Galway, Rory had told Niall where we were going and extended what I assumed was only a polite invitation since he surely didn't want his roommate to hear the crazy we were involved in. Niall had laughed and said, "Why would I want to leave one barren island to go see another?"

I got that now, watching the emerald green broken only by cows, horses, and rocks. What had made these people stay when so many had left? *What makes anyone stay?* I wondered, thinking of Seamus O'Leary. *And what drives you back?* Low stone walls crisscrossed the fields, with houses appearing infrequently, and the sea was nearly always within sight.

*How strange to live,* I mused. Just as Mrs. O'Leary had. With the sea *always* in sight. Unable to escape the constant crash of waves against the shore, the gulls overhead, the sharp sea breeze.

Every so often we had to stop and pull our bikes up against the low stone wall to let a van or a tourist-laden, horse-drawn carriage go by because the roads were that narrow. But before I had time to complain, Aidan happily shouted over his shoulder, "I think this is it!"

If "across the island" was as far as these people ever had to walk, it was a wonder they didn't weigh 300 pounds each.

"That took like five minutes!" Rosie chirped, climbing off her bike beside Aidan.

"It's been twenty," Rory replied crankily.

We stacked our bikes up against the wall of the little whitewashed building with a thatched roof. After all, where was a bike thief going to go?

"Well?" Aidan said, smiling at his brother.

Rory sighed heavily. "Yeah, let's do this."

# *Ceann Coach*
## A DEAD END

THERE WAS A BIT OF A BUZZ INSIDE, WELL, MORE of a murmur, as people sat at various wooden tables arranged around a giant fireplace, everyone relishing the relief from the wind. In the back of the room there was a counter with a cash register that was really more equipped like a home kitchen than a café. We awkwardly lingered by the door until we caught the eye of an old man at a corner table. He gazed at us over the copy of *The Irish Independent* he was holding.

Aidan and I exchanged looks before he marched over to him and the rest of us followed.

"Kieran Browne?"

The man grunted more than anything else, but he did take off his flat cap and lower the paper, which was something.

Aidan smiled despite the cold welcome and took a seat, gesturing for the rest of us to do the same.

"You guys get newspapers out here?" Rosie said with a chuckle.

The man glared at her. He wore round glasses that really gave the air of being "spectacles," and a thick, cream-colored sweater.

"Tough crowd," Rosie muttered, as Aidan cleared his throat.

"I'm sure you're wondering why we wanted to see you," he said, forcing a smile upon his face. "We were actually told about you by Colm Vesey."

The man was silent for a moment, his lips twisting in thought, before he said, "And what do ye want?"

"We, uh, we know how you used to live in Oyster Beach. And you were friends with Seamus O'Leary. And me and my brother here, we're actually his sons. We just found out. And we were told you were with him on the night of the Great Storm and that you …" He looked furtively around before whispering, "We were told you had one of the sealskins."

Not a flicker of emotion passed over the man's face. Not a single flicker. Either he was just in a really bad mood or we were digging up some serious shit he didn't want to deal with.

Rory was looking anxiously around and I longed to reach out and take his hand, to comfort him somehow, but I didn't really think my comfort would be welcome. Not yet. Not until I performed my monologue, the mere thought of which caused my stomach to turn.

"Do you have it?" Aidan prodded.

"No." And he went silent again.

*That's it?* Did he expect us to leave then? Even I was getting annoyed.

"Well do you know where it is?"

The man didn't answer.

"Colm Vesey said you had it. Where. Is. It?"

"I don't know."

"Are you kidding me? It's mine! Tell me where it is!"

"It is with Seamus O'Leary," the man finally said, glancing around to make sure no one was watching. A few people were, but mostly tourists who wouldn't even know what the word "selkie" was if they heard it.

"He's still alive? Where is he?"

"I do not know that."

"I don't believe you! Where is he?"

"You can believe what you like. I do not know where he is, and I really think ye should be leaving. The famous cliffs are just across the road, and those buildings there were in one of your insipid American movies about a romantic Ireland. Go see it, enjoy it. I'm of no use to you." With that, he flipped up his newspaper to cover his face.

"Look," Rosie said in a harsh whisper at the front page, "we know all about the *murder*. I think that means you should talk to us."

"Rosie!" I gasped, as the man lowered his newspaper to gape at her.

"Okay, we're leaving," Rory said, standing up and grabbing the back of his brother's sweatshirt. He pulled him sideways out of his chair and toward the door.

"That isn't fair!" Aidan yelled. "He's obviously lying!"

"C'mon," I whispered at Rosie. She shook her head but got up with me as people watched the spectacle of the shouting American being pushed out the door, the door slamming behind him. As I scrambled after the boys, my cheeks turned red from all the staring eyes. Among them, I found the green ones belonging to the old man at the bike shop. He was watching the scene as he stood from a table near the counter and walked toward Kieran. Embarrassed, I shrugged at him as if to say, "Oh, you know boys." Then I scampered through the door into the cold air.

Outside, Aidan and Rory were involved in a verifiable shouting match.

"I don't give a shit! He's lying!"

"Who the hell cares? You have a family that loves you, why are you hellbent on this stupid mission that's obviously doomed to fail?"

"What happened to our truce to try and understand each other?"

*So* that's *what went on in the shop earlier.*

"I'm trying to, Aidan, but you're making it really difficult! I just don't get it!"

"Leap year," Rosie said happily.

"What?" I turned, and she was pointing across the road at an L-shaped cluster of short, white buildings with thatched roofs. The brightly painted doors, which matched the shutters, were thrown open, with t-shirts and knickknacks on display. There was even a middle-aged woman standing in one of the doorways, watching the bickering brothers with interest, but she looked away when I saw her.

"That old guy is right—that place was in a movie. The movie *Leap Year*. With Amy Adams?"

"Never seen it," I said.

"Oh, well there are some scenes right there," she said, gesturing as she walked over to the patio in front of the buildings which was sprinkled with picnic tables and a lone border collie. "There's this American girl who goes to Ireland to—"

"I don't care!"

We both turned to see Aidan twist and storm away from his brother. I scurried after Rosie to get away from the yelling and instinctively reached a hand out to pet the border collie.

"What's your—"

The dog snarled and Rosie and I both jumped back—right into Rory.

"Oh!"

"Jesus, sorry," Rory said, combing a hand through his hair. He stepped forward and reached toward the dog.

"Be careful—"

Before the admonition was out of my mouth, the dog was turning its head to lean into Rory's hand. *Brat.* I thought of Mrs. O'Leary and her weird affection for Princess. Maybe it was a selkie thing.

"Where did Aidan go?" Rosie asked.

"I don't know," Rory said. Behind him, we could see Aidan stomping off in the direction we'd come. "Off to search the island for a sealskin? To arrange the murder of Kieran Browne? Who knows. But, hey, we're in one of the most popular tourist attractions in Ireland, let's not let him spoil it. You guys want to go see the cliffs?"

"You don't care that Keiran Browne had virtually nothing to say to help?" Rosie asked, her eyebrows quirked skeptically.

Rory shrugged. He didn't; I knew that. He wanted everything to go back to the way it was before Operation Selkie.

"Okay," I said. "Let's go."

# *Tabhartas ó Árainn*
## THE GIFT OF ARAN

"T HE CLIFFS" TURNED OUT TO BE AT THE TOP OF A fifteen-minute hike, so when we arrived at this prehistoric fort—from like 1100 B.C. or something—I was pretty sweaty. It was called Dun Aengus, according to the posters at the entrance to the climb, and Rosie made a not-so-funny joke about beef as we reached the rocky top. Just outside the wall enclosing the fort was a field of jagged rocks sticking upright out of the ground. It was supposed to trip up the horses of intruders and make it more difficult to attack, and I marveled at how easily we walked in now. The thought of these ancient people seeing futuristic tourists walking right into their fort made me giggle.

We squeezed through the opening in the high stone wall, and inside the ring, the wind picked up with a vengeance. The ground here was flat rock interspersed with grass, and though there was another stone wall ahead, the land fell away to the left and you could see ocean for miles. Rosie drifted toward that now, and after overcoming my brief horror that there were no railings or barriers of any kind, I realized this was my chance—finally getting Rory alone and apologizing. As he walked away without a word, my interest in history died away and all I could see was Rory's anguish hidden behind a mask of polite contentment. So I followed him toward the inner wall.

Through a small door-shaped hole in this one, we came to the middle of the fort. A semi-circle stone wall ringed in the cliff, as if nudging visitors toward the perilous edge. Rory just kept on walking.

I hesitated, then followed a few more steps. He stopped within a foot of the edge and sat down on the broken rock floor. It only took a few more shuffled steps of mine before I could see over the edge—and into oblivion.

*Holy crap!*

Just a foot in front of Rory, a sheer drop gave way to hundreds of feet of nothingness, ending far, far below in deep blue waves that crashed over each other in the barbaric Atlantic. The blue stretched on for miles before disappearing in a fog at the horizon. This was truly the horrifyingly epic edge of the earth.

And they couldn't even splurge on some damn rails.

No way was I going any closer.

Everything within me beat as though my very organs were Irish dancing. Gulping, I considered my options. Run away and let this boy go on hating me forever. Or grow up and say sorry for the awfulness

I'd put him through.

*Damn you, conscience.* Why did it have to be here, on the very brink of nothingness?

I'd never considered myself afraid of heights—ferris wheels were a walk in the park—but this. This was insanity.

I forced one more step. Then another. Then I sat down. A good four feet behind Rory.

"Damn it," I breathed. Scooting on my butt, I came almost even to him.

"Holy shit. Holy shit."

He looked over at me with a half-cocked grin.

"All right there?"

"Yeah, yeah, perfectly fine. Just wondering how many tourists they've lost over this thing."

"The Cliffs of Moher are at least twice this high in some places. These are just baby cliffs."

"Well, that's comforting."

We lapsed into silence and while Rory watched the waves, I watched him. Here we were in this heavenly, gorgeous place, and he just seemed … broken.

And then, while I studied the downturn of his eyes, my hand, resting on the rock beneath us, was enveloped by his.

He was holding my hand.

That was it. Here, at the apex of the world, I needed to apologize.

"Rory, I'm sorry."

He didn't look at me, but his eyes climbed from the waves below to the rocky edge right in front of him that, up close, looked entirely benign. You know, until you stepped on it and fell away to nonexistence.

*Focus, Cora.*

"I'm sorry," I repeated. "For everything—the way I left last summer, not emailing you back, the way I showed up this summer. It was really rotten of me, and I just want you to know I didn't do any of it with the intention of hurting you. That's the problem, I wasn't thinking of your feelings—I was thinking of mine. How scared I was to tell you about all this selkie bullshit. I didn't even think about how you'd feel. I mean, this was all about you and your life, your family. I was just selfish. And I think … I think I was scared by how much I liked you. But not emailing you anymore didn't make a difference, I still thought about you every day this year. I'm so sorry, Rory. I never meant to hurt you. But I guess that's what everybody says after hurting a person who doesn't deserve it."

The wind took over my monologue, whipping my words out to sea. I just hoped they had an effect before they disappeared.

"I'm sorry," I murmured again, for good measure.

He nodded before looking at me. "I'm sorry, too. For acting like a brat ever since you got here." He turned to face me, and I put my free hand out, afraid of his proximity to the edge. "I'm really glad you came here, Cora. I was surprised to see Aidan, sure. But I was shocked and excited and nervous, and I guess a little angry, but hopeful, and really confused, when I saw you."

I squeezed his hand, and he squeezed back, his eyes never leaving mine. For the first time since I'd gotten to Ireland, I felt seen, truly *seen* by Rory. The way he'd looked at me last summer, when we'd fallen asleep in cabin 24 and when he'd taken me to see the seal colony and taught me to swim … well, *attempted* to teach me to swim.

"I never stopped thinking about you, either," he said.

The magic words. My fear of this terrifying cliff morphed into an invincible feeling of being able to face anything with this boy by my side.

"I haven't stopped thinking about you since those days you'd sit on the jetty and watch me swim."

My mouth dropped open and Oyster Beach hit me full in the chest. "You knew?"

He chuckled. "Of course I knew. You weren't exactly stealthy. And Princess makes a horrible spy."

"You … you knew all that time? And you didn't think I was a stalker?"

"I didn't care, I thought you were beautiful." He reached a hesitant hand toward a strand of my hair being whipped around by the wind and curled it behind my ear. "Still do."

We were back at the boat around 4:30, before they were even letting passengers on, but Aidan was nowhere to be found. His bike had still been leaning against the café when we went for ours, so we'd walked back, Rory wheeling both his and Aidan's along.

The air had warmed a bit, and it was a wonderful walk, as I thought of all the things I wanted to say to Rory now that we were back on wonderful terms. Like, *I love you*, for one. But Rosie was here, my permanent third wheel.

As happy as I'd been up on that cliff, as we walked down, the distance between Rory and I had seemed insurmountable. He hadn't kissed me, he hadn't held my hand. He hadn't said he still *loved* me. He thought about me, but … why hadn't he kissed me? Did there come a time when thinking about someone wasn't enough?

Back at Browne's Bikes, the man and woman were polite, but eyed us suspiciously. We were probably rather more trouble than most tourists. Neither of the strange old men were anywhere to be found. As we sat on the pier, legs dangling, I watched a dog romp into the waves on the nearby beach, and that image, coupled with Rory's confession about the jetty, brought a nostalgia for Oyster Beach back with a previously unmatched vigor.

I wondered where Lia O'Leary was now. I fully believed there was a creature out there that had once been the Lia I knew. But it scared me to admit that. Because Rory carried the same blood in his veins.

When the boat hands extended the gangplank at 4:40, Rory started to worry. "Should I go looking for him?" he asked.

"There's still twenty minutes left," Rosie said. "He's probably just avoiding you … er, I mean, us. I'm sure he'll be here."

At 4:45, *I* began to worry.

"Maybe you should go looking for him," I said. "What if something happened to him?"

"Hello! We're on a tiny island," Rosie reasoned. "The worst that could happen is he's fallen into a tourist trap."

"That's a lie, you saw those cliffs!" I snapped. "Those were plenty dangerous."

"Yeah, well, we know he wasn't up there."

At 4:50, Rory walked back to the little town to look around. In the distance, I saw him pop into Browne's Bikes, only to leave again moments later. When he returned at 4:55, all the other passengers had boarded.

"Is it okay to worry now?" I snapped at Rosie.

"Yeah, now you can panic."

"What do we do?" I asked, turning to Rory.

He shrugged. "I could give you guys my keys, you guys could go back. I'll hang around here until I find him."

"And sleep on the beach?" Rosie said sarcastically.

"She's right. You should come back with us."

"I'm sure he's capable of taking care of himself. We can come back tomorrow, if he hasn't shown up back in Galway."

Rory shook his head. "No, I can't leave him. Not after everything we've been through. You saw how he's taking it. There's no telling what he'll do. What he's already done."

*Oh God.* What if Aidan *had* done something crazy? He was becoming so increasingly desperate for reasons I couldn't understand. Sure, it was unfortunate how little progress we were making in finding Mr. O'Leary and finding out more about the boys' childhood, but … why was Aidan quite so furious about it all?

"Are you guys coming?"

We all twirled around to find one of the ferry workers watching us, his hand on the gangplank. Another stood on the land side of it, arms braced as if to push.

Rory showed me his phone. Five o'clock on the dot.

*Shit.*

"Yeah, they're coming," Rory said, putting a hand on my back and gently pushing.

"No—"

"Here are my keys." He placed them in my palm as I protested.

"Rory—"

"C'mon, Cora." Rosie pulled on my arm so harshly I stumbled backward.

Rory smiled at me, all at once that boy from last summer wearing that grin that I loved so much. That I'd dreamed of so many times this winter. The corners of his lips were drawn up sharply, his lips taut and revealing just the barest hint of white between them. "I'll be back tomorrow," he said.

"We're setting sail now," the burly worker on the boat shouted impatiently.

I sighed and turned to follow Rosie then stopped on the deck of the boat to watch the burly guy pull in the gangplank with the help of the one on shore. It made a loud scraping noise, and Rory waved at me with a reassuring smile.

"Look!"

Startled, I turned to look were Rosie was pointing down the pier.

"Wait!" I shouted. "Put it back out!"

Aidan was sprinting toward us, his worn backpack bobbing on his back. He looked like a kindergartner who was about to miss the bus. And he was going to be in just as much trouble.

But the burly guy wasn't listening. He was walking away.

"Wait! Wait, you left somebody on shore!"

"Hey!" Rosie sprinted after him, and I watched helplessly as Rory confronted Aidan on land with words I couldn't hear. Rory was gesturing wildly, but Aidan wasn't reciprocating. He just stood there, nodding, a weird grin on his face.

At the sound of scuffling, I turned around to find Rosie spinning in the air as she clutched the back of the burly worker to the sounds of frightened tourists.

"Rosie!" I screamed.

Another worker was dashing to rescue his colleague just as I stumbled over to them.

"Rosie, get off!" I yelled again, tugging on her arm.

"This is the only way I could get his attention," she insisted.

"We just need you to let our friends on," I explained to the worker not currently encumbered by a Rosie shaped chip on his shoulder. "He pulled in the gangplank before they could get on."

"That's not what happened!" the poor burly man yelped.

"Well, yes, it wasn't his fault, they were a little late. But now they're here, and this is the last boat of the day."

"Fine! Fine. We'll let them on," worker number two said. "But ye just earned yourselves a lifetime ban from Aran Ferry." His arm cut across the air for emphasis.

*That's okay*, I thought happily as the man marched over to the gangplank. I'd gotten everything I needed from the Aran Islands.

# Seas Liom
## STAND BY ME

AFTER STOPPING BY THE APARTMENT TO CHANGE, Rory went to work that evening, leaving me on tenterhooks. How had things changed? He had spent most of the ferry ride fuming on the opposite end of the row from his brother, whose goofy smile slowly gave way to his previous grumpy demeanor. But I'd been too blissfully ecstatic to do anything more than daydream. However, now that we were back in the real world, could we pick up where we'd left off last summer?

With Rory gone, my reason returned a little. I was on a roll here, clearing up the debris of my life, and I couldn't stop now. I dialed Dad's cell and he picked up on the first ring.

"Did you tell her?" I asked without preamble.

"Hi, Cora. Yes, I did."

"Are you guys okay?"

"We're fine—"

"No, I mean your marriage. If you've started keeping secrets from Mom—"

"What? Cora, your mother and I love each other very much."

There was a *click* and my mom's anxious voice joined Dad's. "Cora? Are you okay? You were worrying about us?"

"I just … I found a letter about the lawsuit before you even knew and I was afraid … I don't know."

"Honey," Mom's voice was more gentle than I could ever remember it. "We've gone through the most painful thing a couple can go through."

*Gretel.* How stupid of me to think a lawsuit was any sort of challenge to my parents' marriage. It was only then that I understood that I'd underestimated the strength of my parents' love for the entirety of my life.

"We made it through that," Mom said, almost a whisper. "We can make it through anything."

I sniffled in spite of the tough persona I was trying to exude. "Even the downfall of the rainbow shoelace craze?"

Mom giggled, a watery sound. "Yes, darling, even that."

Silence clouded the line, but I welcomed it. Things were okay at home.

"Hey, Dad?"

"Yes, Cora?"

"I'm sorry about everything. It really sucks that this is happening. I know you're great at what you do."

"It's okay. Everything will be okay."

When I got off the phone, I went looking for Rosie. She was watching TV in the sitting room, but Aidan was in there, too, sitting silently in a chair by the windows, staring at the people milling about below.

"Is he okay?" I mouthed, joining Rosie on the couch.

She shrugged. "He hasn't spoken in, like, an hour."

She hadn't bothered to whisper, but Aidan didn't even look at us. His face was somber, and if I wasn't imagining it, a little pale, as his eyes followed people down on the street I couldn't see.

"I'm sorry Kieran Browne couldn't help," I said lamely.

Aidan didn't say anything, but I saw his Adam's apple bob once.

"I don't think it was that he *couldn't* help," Rosie said. "I think he didn't *want* to help."

Watching Aidan's drawn face, I got the feeling this wasn't helping. Time for a change of subject. "How about some dinner? You guys want to get takeout?"

"I ate like twenty of those cookies that taste like Thin Mints," Rosie prattled. "They could give the Girl Scouts a run for their money."

"Aidan?" I asked.

He merely shook his head.

"So what's next for Operation Selkie?" Rosie chirped, as always, oblivious to other people's body language. "Back to the drawing board?"

Aidan finally looked at us. "No," he said. "I'm done."

Rosie and I exchanged a wary glance.

"Just like that?" Rosie asked.

"Yeah, just like that." His head turned back to the windows.

"Um, couldn't we start from square one? I'm sure there's a way to track down Seamus O'Leary."

"He doesn't want to be found," Aidan said.

Rosie scoffed. "That didn't stop you before. What's gotten into you?"

"Rosie!" I hissed. The kid was obviously on the verge of … well, something, though I didn't know what. A mental breakdown? An angry tantrum? A depression? There was no telling. If only Rory were here. Though lately he'd seem to incense his brother more than anything.

"So you're just gonna scurry back to the U.S.?" Rosie asked. "Just give up?"

"I'm just … done," Aidan said again, unhelpfully.

"What the hell does—"

The door opened then and Niall stuck his head in.

"Hey, everybody." He looked around warily; the tension in the room was suffocating. "Rory just texted me, asked me to tell you guys to meet him at The Quays. He's going to play a set after work, and he wants you guys to be there."

The thought of watching Rory onstage again warmed my cheeks. "Thanks," I murmured when it was clear nobody else was going to acknowledge his presence. Rosie was still having a one-sided staring contest with Aidan, who was gazing out the window. With a confused face, Niall left and closed the door behind him.

"Awesome," Rosie said pointedly, glaring at Aidan. "Let's go."

"I'm going to hang around here tonight," he said.

"No you're not," Rosie said.

Aidan looked at her sharply. "Yes, I am."

"Look, I don't know what your problem is, but your brother—your *only* brother from the way you seem to be looking at it—is going to get up in front of a bunch of people and play music. And once you scuttle back home with your tail between your legs, you won't be here to support him anymore. So, yes, you're going. You can sulk about your failed Operation Selkie later."

An uncomfortable silence engulfed the room for a full five seconds.

"You're right," Aidan finally said.

"I am?" she said.

"She is?" I asked.

"What's one last night out? Let's go."

# *Cora*
## CORA

I T TOOK US A WHILE TO GET OUT THE DOOR thanks to Rosie's prolonged makeup regimen now that she was "back on the market"—her disgusting words, not mine. She'd also insisted on dressing me. I fit into one of her looser fitting dresses, cream-colored and silky, which bore a striking resemblance to the dress my mother had picked out for me ages ago.

"Is cream just my color or something?" I said sardonically, twisting to see my butt in the tiny square mirror in Rory's room.

"Definitely," Rosie said. "It makes you look not quite so pale."

"Thanks a lot," I muttered. "Why couldn't blue be my color? Or green or … well anything else? Cream has to be the most boring color on the planet. It's just a nice way of saying 'white.' Which isn't a color. It's the absence of color!"

"White is the presence of all colors, Cora. *Black* is the absence of color."

"My bad. Sorry, Picasso."

"Besides," Rosie plowed on through puckered lips as she slathered on a dark lipstick, "you look hot. Don't argue with the hues that suit you!" Her own dress was tight, bright red, and short. Yeah, maybe cream was okay for me after all. "God, I'm sick of living out of a suitcase." She perched her hands on her hips and turned to look at me, holding her hand out, where a sparkly glob of fake diamonds dangled. "Am I going to get you to wear some chandelier earrings?"

"No!" I yelped, grabbing my earlobe.

"Cora!"

"They're heavy!" I said like a petulant toddler. "They pull on my ears. And while we're at it, I'm not putting any of that on my lips."

"Well, I'm not going to make you," Rosie said with a mischievous grin made all the more roguish by her lipstick.

"Why?"

"Because you're going to be macking on some hottie tonight."

Rolling my eyes I heaved a great sigh. "I don't know about that," I said quietly. Sure, we'd made up. And he'd even called me beautiful. But it wasn't exactly an *I still love you*. He hadn't even kissed me.

"I saw you up on those cliffs, and I know my love connections when I see them."

"That you do, Roz. That, you do."

She forced me into brown woven wedges that were at least a size too big before allowing me out the door.

"C'mon!" I practically yelled at her and Aidan the entire walk down Shop Street. The bar was packed dense as a human jungle by the time we got there, thanks to Rosie's dawdling, but she redeemed herself when she pushed into the bar as confident as ever, expertly whacking aside human limbs to make a path.

"Ow!" a pretty girl in blue gasped. Rosie ignored her.

I usually had better manners, but music was playing over the speakers, and I was desperately hoping we hadn't missed him.

"Which way?" Rosie shouted over my shoulder at Aidan. He pointed to the right, and as we squeezed that way, what had looked like a quaint bar from the outside opened up to a huge space hanging over a floor below, complete with bar, tables, and people holding hands and swaying to the soft music. And across the valley, in a corner that jutted out over the lower level, was the one orchestrating this musical magic.

My breath caught in my throat.

He sat on a stool, strumming away and crooning into a microphone, all alone. None of his bandmates were there today. It was the first time I'd heard him sing. And he was … breathtaking.

"Wow," I breathed, my eyes on Rory but my hand skimming the ornately carved wooden bannister as we descended. Everything in here was ornately carved wood and books and people.

"I don't know this song," Rosie said, crinkling her nose.

Rory had shed his black work polo, and the white tee he wore now strained against his arms as they moved across the guitar. He could have been singing the Barney theme song for all I cared.

I stumbled down the last few stairs, just as Rosie proclaimed, "We're not going to get a table. So let's get drinks."

"We could find a table down there," Aidan said. I briefly glanced to where he was pointing. Another, cozy little downstairs opened up in the corner, belying a whole new level to this place.

"No way," I said. We wouldn't be able to see Rory from there.

Aidan rolled his eyes. "*Hearing* him is enough for me," he said and trotted away.

"Cora! Drinks!" Rosie demanded, waving a hand in front of my face, which was pointed upward as if to soak in the rays of a glorious sun. "Cora!"

But I was paralyzed. Nothing else mattered in the world because I'd just noticed something. The song Rory was singing … it was familiar.

"*As she learns to swim the current of the sea …*"

Not the words, but the melody. I'd heard it once before.

"*… to find passion and survival and a world of independence all her own …*"

That day. In his apartment. When I'd asked him about learning to play the guitar and he'd shut me down with one reference to our failed correspondence. This was *that* song. Slow, rolling, but quick. And, this time, with words.

"*It brought her to me and it changed my heart forever, to know home.*"

His eyes closed briefly, and when they fluttered open, he seemed to be staring into space. I longed for that chocolate warmth to find me in the crowd, but I wasn't even sure he knew we'd made it.

"Here," Rosie said in my ear, shoving a cold glass at me.

"Shh!" I hissed back.

*"The ghosts that follow Cora, make her run a little faster, but she'll always find her way right back to me ..."*

The blood in my veins stopped, taking my heart with it into a dangerous standstill, as Rosie gasped beside me. My knees were no longer reliable and I grabbed at a nearby table for support. It wasn't empty.

"You okay?" a strange, lilting voice asked.

*"The tears she cried, she'll never know, the way they brought the world right to its knees ..."*

"Don't mind her, she's just having a bit of a heart attack," Rosie answered for me. "A good one ... I think."

*"When the cold sets in and Teran rules, she keeps me warm and gives me air to breathe ..."*

Waving my hands at my eyes, I begged the air to work some kind of elemental magic on the water pricking my vision, making Rory, eyes now closed, a watery vision, surreal and ethereal. And, at the moment, I wasn't entirely sure he wasn't a figment of my Mrs. O'Leary-fueled imagination.

*"Fan liom, the banshee wails, as I turn and set my sails, but time stands still for Cora, as she turns the things she touches into gold ..."*

"On second thought, she might be dying, so you might want to call 9-1-1," Rosie said to someone. "Is that a thing here? Or is it a different number? 9-2-5? 8-4-4?"

Big, fat tears—just like the ones in the song—were welling in my eyes, threatening to turn me into a blubbering scene, and I was quickly being depleted of any energy to fight it.

"*And here I stand just on the outside, yes, just waiting for that touch—as the gulls cry and spring tide rolls out to sea ...*"

And then all of a sudden I was bawling. No-holds-barred bawling. I could feel the strangers' eyes on me, the weird chick losing her shit in a public place. But my tear ducts were dying for some space and they were not stopping until I was swimming in my own tears. Rory was accustomed to that, at least. Heck, it had even made it into the song.

Which was slowing now, as Rory's gaze fell to his guitar and he plucked what felt like a final chord. "*As she learns to swim the current of the sea, to find passion and survival and a world of independence ... all her own.*"

Bashfully, he jumped up and set his guitar in a stand next to the stool before heading for the stairs that led down to our level. Applause rang out and a few people whistled, but Rory was looking shyly at the stairs.

"If you could try and pull it together, that'd be great for our public image," Rosie muttered to me. But I had no intentions of holding it together.

I dashed toward the stairs, oblivious to the angry mutters of the people I was knocking into and undoubtedly dousing with their own drinks.

When he saw me, still a few steps away, his face lit up. "You guys did make it! I wasn't sure—"

He didn't have much room to finish that sentence with my lips smashed against his.

I grasped his arms for one frightful moment, but it only took him that long to get over the initial shock and return the kiss, effectively melting everything in me. One of his arms looped around my waist to pull me closer and the other slipped beneath my hair to cup my neck, just as my own looped around his neck and slid into the little cowlick there. It felt just the same—his hair beneath my fingers. He tasted warm and familiar and like the sum of every heart-wrenchingly wonderful dream I'd had that year.

When I registered the fact that there were other people in the world, I realized they were clapping. Hoots and hollers and whistles echoed around us but I was too far gone to pull back.

"I think we've lost our guitarist for the night," a man said through the loudspeaker. That was met with a resounding laugh, and I smiled into Rory's lips. "I guess I'll play you some tunes then."

Rory finally pulled away, but cupped my face in his hands. "So you liked the song, then?"

My giggle turned into a bit of a snort. "It was the single most beautiful thing I've ever experienced in my life."

"I couldn't find a song with your name in it, so I had to write one." He smirked, just a bit of white peeking out between his lips, which I couldn't pull my eyes from.

Above us, music began to play and Rory glanced up. Following his gaze, I found a man strumming Rory's guitar to a fast, jolly tune.

"*Well, I took a stroll on the old long walk, of a day-I-ay-I-ay!*" The entire room boomed as everyone sang along.

"I was going to play 'Ain't No Mountain High Enough' next," Rory said as I giggled. "But I guess I got outvoted. This is a popular song, Galway Girl. Shall we?" He stepped back and extended one hand, bowing slightly.

It was now or never. *Stop being a coward, Cora.* I was perfectly aware—and ashamed—that I'd spent the whole year being a scaredy-cat and broken the heart of the only boy I'd ever loved. But I'd finally found some courage and flown across the Atlantic to face him. Only to spend the following days stumbling around Ireland like a yellow-bellied mouse once again. It was time I took action just as bold and brilliant as getting on that plane had been.

"I love you!" I shrieked.

Several people turned to cast frightened looks my way, but the only pair of eyes I could see crinkled up with a smile. "I love you, too, Galway Girl." Pressing a kiss to my forehead, he grabbed my hand and pulled me to the middle of the dancing mass of people where I twirled around him. I wasn't a big dancer, but for some reason, tonight, there was an energy inside me begging to escape. My inner ballerina was madly in love and the only way it could come out was by swaying and bouncing and laughing hand in hand with the boy I loved.

Rosie appeared beside us, dragging Aidan with her. For a moment his face was threatened by a frown, but then he smiled at me and his brother and consented to half-heartedly twist his hips as she bumped and grinded all over him to the appalled looks of the Irish around her.

"What? You guys don't grind?" Rosie asked, not letting that stop her one bit.

"Rory?"

"Mmm?" He spun me around in an old-fashioned gesture.

"There was Irish in your song, wasn't there?

"*Fan liom.*" He pronounced it *fin lum.*

"What does it mean?" I asked.

He grinned. "Wait for me."

# Cuireadh
## AN INVITATION

ON THE WAY HOME, RORY CONVINCED US THAT a walk on the beach was mandatory. Of course I was in no mood to deny him that, but Aidan looked annoyed. Rosie was drunk enough to drag him along despite my desperate eye signals that it would be perfectly alright if they went home. No such luck.

As we walked down the street on the Claddagh side of the river, Rory pointed out the big orange and brown boat with unfortunately red and white trim. "The sign's gone."

Sure enough, the big mast was blank, devoid of any advertisement for the sale of the craft.

"It sold." Rory sounded almost disappointed.

"Were you planning on b-buying a boat?" Rosie piped up with a hiccup.

"No," Rory said wistfully. "Guess I just didn't expect

it to sell."

"Look, it's a full moon," Rosie said, pointing. The big moon hung over the water, reflecting back at itself with a mighty glow.

"It's finally full," I said quietly, so only Rory could hear me. "You know what that means."

"Spring tide."

Having noticed our quiet, private conversation, Rosie hustled to a jog. "Wait up!" she shouted at Aidan, who was walking ahead of us, his hands in his pockets. He'd been aloof all night, but not quite so cranky as I'd grown accustomed to. He paused at the boat graveyard, but shook his head to himself and walked on.

"He seems really upset about Kieran Browne turning out to be a dud," I said.

"Yeah," Rory agreed. "Who knows what absurd idea he'll cook up next."

"Actually, earlier, while you were at work, he said he was done looking. That he was giving up."

Rory looked at me suspiciously. "He did?"

I nodded. "Yeah, he was all down about it. Rosie kind of yelled at him to get him to come out tonight. He finally agreed; he was like 'what's one last night out?'"

"But his return ticket isn't for another few weeks."

I shrugged. "Probably plans on moping about for the rest of the trip. Or changing his ticket."

Rory shook his head. "I don't know what's going on with him. He's not usually like this."

Ahead, Rosie and Aidan were cutting across a field toward the path that followed along the sea. On a whim, I tugged Rory's hand to pull him away from them, to the left. The boat graveyard stretched out along the river, boat after decrepit boat.

It was dimly lit by the lights from the city across the river, but I could see Rory's smile.

Stopping by a pile of empty lobster pots, I leaned against the side of a blue boat with a tiny wheelhouse that was caving in. My plan was to work up the courage to kiss him again, but for some reason I was more nervous now that we were all alone. I gulped, searching for something to say, but Rory spoke first.

"Speaking of return tickets …" A little grin lifted the corner of his mouth, but he wasn't looking at me. His fingers were picking at the chipping paint behind my head. Was he nervous too?

"Yeah?" I prompted.

"Well, I was thinking … you could stay a little longer. I mean, after Aidan and Rosie go back to the U.S. You could extend the trip a little. If you wanted."

A grin broke through my nervousness. Staying with Rory—alone? The idea was nerve-racking, but exhilarating. Without Rosie or Aidan around, I could finally break through this nervousness and get to know Rory—get to know *us*, who we were *together.* Rory's deep brown eyes searched mine for a moment before nervously retreating back to the pesky paint. *Learn to live a little, Manchester*—I could just imagine Rosie's advice.

"I think I'd like that," I murmured.

"I know you have the job and everything—"

"Something tells me I could get a little more time off." Let's face it, I was more a mopey thorn in their side—pun intended—than an actual help.

He nodded, his grin growing. "Okay then. We could get a bunch of lilies and irises and rhododendron flowers so you can practice your arranging skills, keep up your talents in your absence."

"Okay, rhododendron? And the other day you said 'Gerbera Daisy'! Since when do you know so much about flowers?"

His eyes flicked to the ground, his smile disappearing. "You told me in one of your first … well, only, emails that you got a job at a flowershop. I may or may not have studied up on different kinds of flowers so we could talk about your job and stuff."

Before I knew it, my fingers were searching out that cowlick at the back of his neck, and my lips were on his. He reacted immediately this time, pulling me tight against him, his hands on my back.

"Wait." I pulled away, breathless. "I forgot—I'll have to talk to my parents about staying. They're going through a lot right now, what with the lawsuit and everything."

His eyebrows fell. "Oh yeah"—his breath was ragged, too—"I'm sorry about that."

I shrugged, playing it off as nothing, as if we got sued everyday. "Dad doesn't seem extremely worried, so I'm trying not to be. Besides, I don't think they'd mind whether I'm there or not. Would probably be easier for them if I wasn't." My breath hadn't caught up from the last kiss when I leaned in for another.

This time he was tender, and his hands cupped my cheeks. He pulled his lips away after only a moment with a great sigh. "I can't believe you came back."

"Back? I've never been to Ireland." I chuckled. This close to his face, I had the most astounding view of his brown eyes, which I was sure held depths I could now only imagine. But I couldn't wait to dive into them after Rosie and Aidan left.

"Back to me."

"Yes, you can. You knew all along."

His brows quirked. "What do you mean?"

"It was in your song. 'But she'll always find her way right back to me.' *Fan liom.*"

He laughed, his hands still warm on my face.

"Did I butcher the pronunciation?" I asked.

"Only a little. But you're right. I guess deep down, I did know all along. Or it was wishful thinking."

He kissed the tip of my nose and my whole body thrilled under the touch. Before I could move the kiss to our lips, he went on.

"Speaking of wishful thinking."

"Yeah, I wish Ireland had Taco Bells, too."

He laughed loudly. "Of all the things to wish for? *Taco Bell?* The things I don't know about you, Cora Manchester! I would pick Arby's over Taco Bell any day!"

I scoffed playfully. "That is absurd—"

"Wait!" A big smile was plastered across his face, his brown eyes sparkling with the light of the full moon or the lights behind me or the light inside him, I wasn't sure. "I'm about to do something that I *think* is really romantic, so please stop talking about fast food."

My heart flip-flopped. "Okay."

He stuffed a hand in the pocket of his hoodie. "So, last fall, when I still thought you were into me—"

"Rory! I am—"

"Sh, sh!" He pressed a finger on his free hand to my lips with a smile. "I know that now, of course. But back when—oh, forget the speech. Here." He pulled his hand out of his pocket and held it out to me, revealing a small red velvet bag with a gold rope pull around the top.

"What is it?" I breathed.

"You'll see in 2.5 seconds if you open it."

My eyes met his, which were still shining brilliantly, and then I grabbed it as unceremoniously as humanly possible. *So much for romance, Cora.*

Pulling open the top, I tipped it upside down and a silver ring fell into my palm.

*A Claddagh ring.* The ring's miniature heart was held by two minuscule hands. The heart was ruby-red and wore a perfect, tiny crown.

"I bought it last fall," Rory explained, "when I first got here, from one of the shops that claims to be the original maker of the Claddagh ring. There are a couple that say that, who knows which is telling the truth. Anyway, I was going to mail it to you, but ..."

But then I'd shattered his heart into a trillion shards.

Gulping back my emotions, I slipped it on my finger. It was a bit big for my ring finger, but slid perfectly onto the middle.

"I know it's not Tiffany's or anything, but—"

"It's better."

The little boat rocked precariously as I pulled him toward me by the front of his hoodie.

If only the fates could have gotten on board with me being so blissfully happy for once. But, as time always tells, they weren't.

# *Tá an Rún Scaoilte*
## THE SECRET'S OUT

WHEN WE GOT HOME, I FOLLOWED ROSIE BACK to Rory's room, where she flopped on the bed, her arms splayed. "I'm so tired!" she said with a yawn.

"Is that why you were so quiet on the walk home?" She and Aidan had barely spoken the entire way.

"No, that was because you two lovebirds wouldn't have heard if I'd climbed up onto the Oscar Wilde statue and screamed," she said sardonically.

A grin took over my face, and she soon followed suit. "I'm sorry," I said, probably not looking all that sorry.

"So what happened?" she squealed, sitting up. "Dish!"

"I don't kiss and tell," I said with a grin.

"Oh my *God!* Cora, you *so* love him!"

With a smile so big it felt like my face was going to split in two, I shoved my hand into her face.

"Oh my God!" she screeched, yanking my hand even closer to peer at my brand new Claddagh ring. "It's beautiful!"

"Hush!" I scolded.

"I need *details*, Manchester!"

"Okay, I will, but let me brush my teeth and stuff first. And say good night to everybody. We can dish before sleep."

Rosie groaned. "But I want to hear about you and Selkie Boy macking!"

"Okay, one, do not call him that. At least not where he can hear you. And two, just wait a minute!" After digging my toothbrush out of my bag, I threw Rosie's backpack at her. "Go brush your teeth while I go seek a good night kiss."

Rosie let the bag hit her in the stomach, pursing her lips and making kissing noises as she toppled over. "Of course, I'll give you a good night kiss, Manchester!"

Rolling my eyes, I headed for the hallway.

"What? Do selkies kiss better than humans or something?" she shouted after me.

After pulling the door shut before Rory or Aidan could hear my rude best friend, I made my way down the hall to the sitting room and rapped gently on the door.

"Come in."

Rory was alone inside, bending over one of the couches to make himself a bed out of a few blankets.

"Hey," I said, my brilliant conversation skills shining through.

"Hey," he said with a grin.

"I—uh, I just came to say good night." Rooted to my spot by the door, I realized this was a bit of a stupid idea, as I didn't have anything else to say.

Luckily, Rory took over the situation. "Well then, good night, Cora." He closed the distance in three quick strides and looped his arms around my back as I chided myself.

*You should have brushed the teeth* before *this, Cora!*

Before I had much more time to regret my choices, he bent his head to kiss me.

Just one short, quick press of the lips was enough to get my heart buzzing, and my lips followed his for a moment as he pulled away. He chuckled and I opened my eyes in time to see the amusement in his face.

"What? I wasn't done yet," I said quietly.

He rubbed a knuckle against my cheek. "This is shaping up to be the best summer ever."

"I'll call my parents tomorrow."

"And I'll call mine. I have about a million missed calls from my mom." He kissed the tip of my nose. "Good night, Miss Manchester."

"Good night, Mr.—" And here, just as I was about to say "O'Brien," I had the realization that in a former life, he was, just like Seamus, an "O'Leary." But then I realized saying so aloud would only make him sad, but by this time I'd paused too long and his smile faltered as he saw everything going on in my head as plainly as if I'd written it down. "… Rory," I finished lamely.

Flustered, I turned and bolted, and my hand was on the door

handle to Rory's room when I remembered my toothbrush. I was gripping it so tightly there would surely be a toothbrush-shaped imprint in my palm for the foreseeable future. Turning, I walked quickly back down the hall to the bathroom, berating myself all the way.

*Stupid, stupid!* Why did I have the uncanny ability to always mess up everything in my life that even resembled perfection?

My hand was on the knob to the bathroom when I heard noise inside. It was the distinct sound of someone sacrificing their dinner to the porcelain god.

*Shit.* Could Rosie have been wrong about the pregnant thing? Without thinking, I twisted the knob and stepped inside, my hand already raised to pull her hair back out of harm's way.

"Oh, Roz—"

It wasn't Rosie.

"Oh shit, I'm so sorry—" I backed two steps out of the room, pulling the door closed, before I registered what I was seeing. Then I froze, half in, half out of the room.

"Cora," Aidan said, his voice thick and cracking. He looked up at me from the toilet bowl, which he was hugging like a teddy bear.

"I'm sorry, I didn't mean to barge in, I thought you were Rosie." I paused. "Are ... are you feeling alright?"

He shrugged. "Guess I had too much to drink."

The only problem was I hadn't seen Aidan with a drink all night long.

"Don't tell my brother, okay? He'd be mad ... I, uh, got so drunk."

# *Briseadh Isteach ar Phlean*
## A PLAN INTERRUPTED

I 'D KEPT INFORMATION FROM RORY BEFORE AND IT had not only turned into one of the worst years of my life, but it had nearly ruined everything. Thank God he'd forgiven me, but I wasn't about to do it again. Instead, I burst into the sitting room.

"What's the matter?" Rory asked, taking in my face as he sat up from where he lay on the couch, making Rex groan in annoyance.

"I … uh … I think you should come here," I said.

"Why? What happened?" Rory stood and following me out of the room.

"It's Aidan." I stopped outside the closed bathroom door and jabbed my finger at it.

The sound of retching traveled through the wood, and Rory blanched. Diving for the door, he wrenched it open.

Aidan looked up and rolled his eyes. He spit into the toilet then grunted, "Shortest kept secret in the history of mankind, Cora."

Rory disappeared and returned moments later with a bucket. He stepped into the bathroom, helped Aidan up by the arm, and flushed the toilet. "Living room. Now."

Hunched over the bucket like it was the source of life itself, Aidan trotted into the living room and plopped down on the couch. Rex snuggled up to his side and commenced snoozing.

Rory followed, his face angry as a storm, and I wasn't sure whether I should be present for whatever conversation followed. But Rosie appeared then in the doorway.

"What's going on?" she asked, taking in Aidan, the bucket, and Rory's face fit for murder.

"What's going on?" Rory repeated. "What's going on is that my little brother appears to be ill and has failed to inform me of this."

"Oh boy." Rosie walked straight to the couch and sat beside Aidan, a hand going to his back, which she rubbed comfortingly.

"Well?" Rory demanded when Aidan refused to speak.

"Well what?"

Rory crossed his arms over his chest. I wanted to go to him and rub his back comfortingly, too, but I was rooted to my spot in the middle of the room. "Are you sick?" he asked, his voice even, measured.

"Obviously," Aidan said.

"That's not what I mean and you know it!" Everything was quiet for a moment, before Rory whispered into the silence, "Did you have a relapse?"

"Yes," Aidan said.

Rory's eyes fell shut and his shoulders dropped like all the air had left his body.

All I could hear in the silence was the muffled sound of people on Shop Street outside the closed windows and Rex's soft snores. The room felt stuffy and I longed to go open a window, to let in the fresh air *and* the noise to dispel this tension. But even Rosie knew better than to speak or act now.

"Do Mum and Dad know?" Rory finally asked, standing dejectedly in front of the couch, his arms hanging limply by his sides. He'd never looked so helpless to me.

Aidan shook his head.

"How?"

"I was sick for a while, so they made me go to the doctor. There were some tests done at the hospital … that's where I ran into Mr. Hall. He was there for some treatment, and that's when he told me … everything. Decided to give me the sealskin, which, unfortunately, turned out to be yours. I think he felt sorry for me or something, knew I was dying."

Every organ in my body twisted and I really wasn't sure I could take another breath. Was Aidan really *dying?*

"How do Mum and Dad not know?" Rory repeated.

"I'm eighteen now, so they let me go back for the results by myself. The results weren't good. But I told Mum and Dad it was bronchitis."

Rory covered his face with his hands.

"You are such an idiot," Rosie said softly, her hand still rubbing Aidan's back.

"Why didn't you tell them?" Rory demanded.

"Why? It would only upset them."

"Are you insane? You think when they find out they won't be furious?"

"They're not going to find out."

"What are you talking about? Of course they're going to find out. In about ten seconds, when I call them."

Aidan was quiet, but Rory was too worked up to wait for an answer.

"I can't believe you! Is this why you've been so desperate to find Seamus O'Leary? You think your days are numbered, so you have this death wish to meet your birth father?"

"Rory!" Rosie gasped at the same time Aidan said, "No."

"We can beat this," Rory said harshly.

"That's not why," Aidan said.

"You've beat it before," Rory said.

"You're not listening to me!" Aidan's voice reached a volume I'd never heard from his mouth before. His voice sounded strange and unfamiliar at that decibel. "I said no, that's not why I've been so desperate."

"Then why?"

"I'm gonna go back."

"Back?" Rosie repeated.

"To the sea."

It felt as though the earth itself had stopped its rotation in pure shock.

"What are you talking about?" Rory asked in a voice so low, it was almost inaudible.

"*That's* what I was worried about. Finding the sealskin. Not finding Seamus. I ... would have ... liked to meet him again, but there's nothing he can do for me now. I just wanted my sealskin so I could turn back."

"Shut up." His voice was still in that frighteningly low pitch, and this time it was trembling. "I don't know why you're messing with me, but I've had enough. Of all of this. Of the crazy search, of your twisted need to feel close to these people."

"I'm not joking, Ronan!"

"Don't you *dare*!" Rory nearly screamed.

"Rory," Aidan said, gentler this time, undaunted by his brother's screaming. "Think about it. This body of mine is broken. Who's to say, if I changed back into a seal, I wouldn't be perfectly healthy?"

"Aidan, we'll get through this. We have—"

"You don't know what you're talking about, Rory."

"Yes, I do. I was there—"

"No, you don't!"

Tears were pricking at my eyes, but I didn't dare let them fall for fear of the noises that were threatening to strangle my throat. I wouldn't be the one to break this silence. Rosie's hand was back in her lap now, I noticed, and she was staring at her clasped hands.

"I don't want to go through it again," Aidan said, his voice fuming. "I don't want to. Did you ever imagine how that was for me? What that was like? The treatment that nearly kills you? I don't want to go through that again, Rory. I'd rather ..." He gulped, as if realizing whatever he was about to say would only injure his brother further.

After a long moment, a smile stretched across Aidan's face and he added, "Besides, haven't you ever wondered? What it's like? Going back?"

"No," Rory said sternly.

"I know that's not true." Aidan's voice didn't hold anger any longer. I could see the little crooked tilt of his front tooth and it made him look so very young. "We've both wondered. It's impossible not to. And I want to find out. We have this incredible opportunity, and I'm going to seize it."

"We don't know how it works, Aido." There was genuine fear in Rory's eyes now. "We have no idea how it works. It would be more of a suicide mission than staying here in your body."

My mind instantly went to the night Rory had touched his sealskin. We did know a *little* about how it worked. Glancing at Rory's hand now, I saw the red welt was still there, just a ghost of what it was before. But he apparently had no intention of letting Aidan in on that secret.

"That's not, strictly speaking, true," Aidan said. "Think about it—this stupid body of mine has been failing me my whole life. There's not a great chance I'll make it very far. But we know aging works differently for selkies. If I go away and my body there is healthy, then I could come back in-in, like, thirty years. Rory, I could see your children!"

Rory gulped and shook his head, his lips twisted up in an effort to keep at bay whatever emotions were racking him. "Thank God we didn't find the other skin," Rory said softly. "Just what did you intend to tell Mum and Dad? Or were you just going to leave without saying anything? Leave me to pick up the pieces?"

Aidan shrugged. "Whatever they'd think would be better than watching me die."

"I cannot believe we're having this conversation. Where did my little brother go? The normal one? The one who behaved all the time and loved his mum and dad and made me look like a jerk by the sheer tenacity of his goodness? Where did that guy go?"

"He turned into a selkie," Aidan said with a grin.

Rory shook his head angrily and moved to the table in the corner of the room. "I-I can't have this conversation any longer." He picked up his cell and started dialing. "Go to bed, Aidan. Sleep in my room. I'm calling Mum and Dad. We'll continue this nightmare in the morning."

"Rory—"

"Don't even try," Rory said, holding up a hand. As he lifted the phone to his ear, Aidan dry heaved into the bucket. Rosie rubbed his back again and flashed a look at me that said *Holy shit!*

Widening my eyes, I nodded in agreement.

"Shit," Rory said, taking his phone away from his ear. "It's only like 10:30 there. Are they seriously asleep?"

Five attempts later, it was decided that Mr. and Mrs. O'Brien were not going to be reached.

"You don't have to tell them," Aidan said, his voice amplified in the bucket.

"And what? Let you stick around here puking up your guts and running around the countryside until you find that stupid sealskin? Not gonna happen. Go to bed, Aidan."

"Come on," Rosie said, standing. "I'll tuck you in. And sleep next to you, if you don't mind. I don't wanna sleep on the floor."

Aidan let her pull him up by the arm, and as they turned for the door I realized just how wretched Aidan's face looked. This was tearing him apart, too.

When they were gone, I turned back to Rory, who was standing by the bank of windows, staring down at the street. Pulling on his arm, I got him to turn to me before pressing my head to his chest and wrapping my arms around his waist. His heart beat frantically beneath my cheek.

"Jesus Christ," Rory muttered.

"I know."

He rested his cheek on my head and folded his arms around my back.

"I'm so sorry," I said. "I'm so so sorry."

"I can't even ..." Rory let out a long sigh. "I just ... I can't believe I didn't suspect that. He just ... he's never lied to me about anything before. I didn't ... I didn't think he could ever ... do something like that."

*Times are a'changing, brother,* Aidan had said to Rory on our first night in Ireland. Oh boy, I could never have guessed just how much he meant that.

"It's spring tide," I whispered into his shirt.

I could feel him shake his head on top of mine. "Thank God we never found the third sealskin."

# *Rabharta*
## SPRING TIDE

W HEN I WOKE UP, I WAS TANGLED IN RORY'S arms on the couch and the gentle tapping of a light rain was falling on the windows. My neck hurt indescribably, but the euphoria of waking up in Rory's arms nearly outweighed the pain. But then everything from the previous night came flooding back to me.

Rory groaned. Opening one eye, he saw my face and attempted a grin that just came out lackluster and sad. "Man, I was hoping yesterday was a dream." He closed his eyes. "More like a nightmare."

"There's something tickling my toes," I said. As I pulled the blanket away, Rex popped his head up and looked at me through groggy eyes. Annoyed, he hopped down from the couch and nearly landed on Rory's phone, which was blinking on the floor next to the couch. "I think your parents called back."

He sighed. "I should go wake Aidan up. We need to call them back and sort through this."

Just then there was a knock on the living room door. Self-conscious, I sat up and scooched a little away from Rory.

"Come in!" he called.

Niall poked his head into the room and Rex gave one happy bark and darted through his legs to go do a morning around-the-apartment romp. "Hey. Thought I heard the sounds of people waking up."

"Just barely," Rory said with a yawn.

"I, uh, just wanted to let you know I ran into your brother earlier."

"What?" Rory shot up and spun to face his roommate. "He's awake?"

"Yeah, he was out here a couple hours ago." Niall jabbed a thumb over his shoulder toward the hall. "He asked me to tell you he was going down to the boat graveyard. I don't know what that is, but—"

"I do," Rory said. "He hasn't come back?"

Just then Niall stumbled forward with a yelp. "Is Aidan in here?" Rosie asked, her hair a mess. "He's not in the bed."

"He went to the boat graveyard," I said.

"What's that?" Rosie asked.

"This place down by the Claddagh."

Rory looked panicked as he spun around the room looking for his shoes. "What on earth is he doing? He can't do anything without the skin, right? You don't think he'd … do something drastic?"

He stopped and looked at both Rosie and me in turn. All at once we sprang into action. I dove for my shoes and Rory grabbed the hoodie he'd shed yesterday, finally finding his shoes under the table, as Rosie retrieved hers from the bedroom.

"What's going on?" Niall asked helplessly.

Nobody answered, as we were already halfway out the door.

The rain soaked my dress, which I'd never changed out of last night, and I was shivering long before we reached the end of Shop Street and crossed over the river to dart toward the boat graveyard.

Aidan was nowhere to be seen.

"Aidan?" Rory called, walking right up to the edge of the water.

Rosie and I split, walking opposite ways through the tangle of broken boats. "Aidan?" I called. In front of me, the promenade turned to curve along the beach of Galway Bay, but it was nearly empty. The rain was growing heavier and heavier, and most of the people who were about were moving quickly to get out of the rain.

"You guys?" I heard Rosie's tentative voice. Turning, I saw her a few yards behind me. She twisted and pulled something out of an old green boat. It was a pile of clothes.

"No! No! No! Aidan!" Rory splashed into the water, and I ran for Rosie, who was beginning to cry into the t-shirt folded neatly on top of a blue hoodie and a pair of jeans.

Bending over the boat, I searched through the junk inside—tangled fishing net, rusted metal things, and years of rotting wood—but I wasn't sure what I was looking for.

"Cora?" Turning, I watched Rosie pull her hand out of the jeans pocket, a folded square of paper between her fingers. "To Rory, Cora, and Rosie," she read aloud from the scribble on the front.

"Rory!" I screamed, grabbing the paper from her hands and unfolding it with shaking fingers. He was knee-deep in the ocean, but turned at my cry and stumbled back to us, as my eyes flew over the hastily written words and the ink leaked and ran in the rain.

*Hey guys,*

*As you've probably guessed by now, I'm gone! I know you're going to be mad, Rory, but you have to trust me. I'll see you again, I promise.*

*You need to go see Mr. O'Leary. He's on Inis Mor, working at Browne's Bikes. He was at the bike shop that day we were there and even at the café with Kieran Browne. Kieran promised not to tell us anything, but then Seamus saw my little temper tantrum outside and came after me, told me who he was. We talked for a long time, Rory, I told him everything, and he agreed with me that I was running out of options. He gave me the sealskin.*

*I know you don't agree, but I think some day you will. I love you, Rory. You're my best friend. And I hope, by the time I see you again, you'll understand why I did this.*

*I've mailed a letter to Mum and Dad that explains everything. You know, the version where I decided I wanted to travel the world and found our birth mother in Germany. I hope you don't feel like I've left you to pick up the pieces, I tried to clear them up as best I could before I left.*

*Cora and Rosie, you can't believe how grateful I am that I didn't have to do this alone. Take care of Rory, okay? Hope to see you guys when I get back. Can't wait to tell you all about it!*

*And Rory, please, please go see Seamus. I told him to expect you, and he agreed to talk to you about everything. He even has one of Mrs. O'Leary's old diaries. Learn everything you can about them. They're good people. They're our people.*

*See you soon, big brother.*


*Love,*

*Fionn*

*But you know me as Aidan*

TO BE CONTINUED...

The final book of the *Hearts Out of Water* series,
*The Last Secret*, is available now!

# ACKNOWLEDGMENTS

As usual, I need to thank: My mom and dad, for their unending support (and nagging to "go write!"). Michael, my own Irish dream guy who cooks dinner and puts up with my many and varied writing moods (and knows which ones require chocolate). My brother, for graciously letting me be the baby of the family (as if he had a choice). My book-loving aunts and uncles and cousins, who are numerous enough to support a writing career alone, especially Joe and Cathy O'Brien, who are my constant supporters. My favorite Rottweiler mix, Lucy, and a special Irish dog named Rex, for snuggles.

Also thanks to all the Incarnate Word Academy Red Knights who showed tremendous support when *Learning to Swim* (*All the Tales We Tell*) came out. I couldn't have picked a better place to spend my teenage years!

Oh, and thanks to my brilliant Irish language translator, Kevin Ó Maolalaigh, a true Connemara man who never tires of translating seemingly meaningless and endless words and phrases for me. Irish is a beautiful language, but dang is it confusing!

Last but definitely not least: a very special thank you, thank you, thank you to all the readers and bloggers who posted reviews in the early days of book one. Truthfully, your reviews, messages, and stars were what convinced me to keep going, proving that readers truly are a special kind of people!

# ABOUT THE AUTHOR

A short, dog-obsessed, ketchup-loving romantic from the middle of the U.S., Annie Cosby spent three years living in Galway, Ireland, which gave her mono, set her soul on fire, and introduced her to her husband.

She is the author of the *USA Today*-recommended *Hearts Out of Water* and *Souls Out of Ireland* series, the Amazon-chart-soaring *Humming Song Saga,* and countless other tales seeped in Celtic lore.

She now lives in St. Louis, Missouri, with a Rottweiler mix named Lucy and her favorite Irishman.

Sign up for her Readers Club and find more bookish fun at AnnieCosby.com.

# BOOKS BY ANNIE COSBY

**HEARTS OUT OF WATER**

*All the Tales We Tell*

*Lifespan of a Memory*

*The Last Secret*

*Fadó, Fadó: Selkies, Kelpies and Other Celtic Creatures*
(A Companion Collection to Hearts Out of Water)

**SOULS OUT OF IRELAND**

*The Daughters of Morrigan*

**THE HUMMING SONG SAGA**

*Daughter of the Diamond King*

www.ingramcontent.com/pod-product-compliance
Lightning Source LLC
Chambersburg PA
CBHW051645180726
48284CB00006B/1871